KELEA'S GIFT

KELEA'S GIFT
Surf Stories

Chris Ahrens
Chubasco Publishing Company

Chubasco Publishing Company
P.O. Box 697
Cardiff-by-the-Sea
California, USA 92007

Manufactured in the United States of America

Cover painting and design by Michael Cassidy

ATTENTION ANAL-RETENTIVES:
EARN BIG- MONEY WHILE WORKING AT HOME!
The first person to correctly identify a spelling error in this volume
will receive my personal check for twenty-five cents.

— Chris Ahrens,
Chubasco Publishing Company

DEDICATION

To my Aunt Bea, who, in 1961, suggested that I get a Velzy Surfboard. To my wife, Tracy, who has read and reread every word and laid out every page of our four books. To my parents, who took me surfing and made me lunch and who were patient during the gremmie years. To my favorite gremmie, Stuart Grauer. To Chrissy and Ray. To Susan Lazear. To Chuck and Nancy Powers for raising children who will change the world. To all underdogs, including Jaime and Antonio. To this world's losers, many of whom will be kings in the next. To Carl and Denise Ekstrom, congratulations and have a wonderful life. To Yo Mama. To Jim, Becky, Michael, Sherri and Damon. To Peter Saint Pierre and the entire Moonlight gang. To John and Judy Montague. To Henry Hester. To Dennis Wills, the world's greatest dumpster surfer. To Billy Moore and Pastor John Ringgold who taught me that "I'm too blessed to be stressed." To "Murph The Surf" and the boys. To the Sea Hags. To Eric Villanueva, who died from the polluted waters of Malibu, because people still flush their waste into the ocean. And to Syrus King—see you on the other side.

✦

Special Thanks to: Kimberly Havas, Christine Hopkins, Michael Cassidy, John Patrick Kennedy, Donald Takayama, Roy McKay, Wade Koniakowsky and Big Bang.

Subject to the moon, to the stars, to the influence of the light of other worlds, she changed her moods and appearance in a way that I thought fantastic, but it was as fatal as the tide.

—Octavio Paz, 1949
My Life with the Wave

CONTENTS

CONTENTS

KELEA'S GIFT

INTRODUCTION
500 Years of Free Surfing

My father was a surfer, defined as much by the one hundred pound wooden surfboard that he borrowed on occasion, as by the way he lived. He rode Santa Monica through the Depression and Prohibition, spending entire weeks camped out on the sand, spearing corbina in the shore break before cooking them over a wood fire. Other methods of survival included bare fisted boxing matches with friends. The last man standing would collect his five dollar prize, and hobble to the market to purchase enough groceries for everyone, including the loser, for the week. On certain evenings, Dad and his friends would swim to one of the speakeasy party boats anchored three miles offshore, slam a drink or two, and swim back to the beach, in their trousers, in the dark. They bodysurfed, lifted weights, wrestled and went straight off on those long wooden planks, once or twice, even at Malibu.

As a child, my father's surf stories held little interest for me. Toy trains were my deal, and I had my HO set up on a piece of plywood in the family den. The only thing I liked better than trains were movies, and every Saturday afternoon, my partner in the train, Robert Vermont, and I would abandon our hobby and attend the Garmar Theater. One Saturday matinee featured the movie, *Gidget*. Before the credits had even finished rolling, we had run home to rip the tracks from their plywood base. Within minutes we had cut the train's foundation in two, painted both halves of the wood yellow, and scrawled our first names on our "boards" in red paint. The next weekend was spent at the beach, where we were disappointed to discover that our boards didn't float, and that we had built a pair of ankle smacking skimboards.

It would be two more years before I rode a real surfboard. Then began the era of Dad carting my younger brother, David, and I around to breaks from 22nd Street in Hermosa Beach, clear down south, to Swami's in Encinitas.

When we expressed annoyance at increasing crowds in the surf, Dad told us about a place where the surf was good all day long, and there were never more than three or four people in the water at one time. The next weekend, we drove north through Santa Monica, past Topanga, arriving at the point break that I recognized from the magazines as Malibu. Dad pulled over and stood at the side of the road, his head darting back and forth quizzically, looking for something that was no longer there. His quiet paradise of the '30s had become everybody's noisy purgatory of the '60s. I counted over one hundred surfers in the water. To my recollection, not one of them was a girl.

When I finally inherited Dad's '59 Biscayne, I wore through countless sets of retreads on a quest that took me from San Francisco to Baja, concentrating primarily on the breaks between Seal Beach and Trestles. I met a great many surfers and even more hodads. And while a girl, Gidget, had sent us to the sea in the first place, and was at least partially responsible for the surf boom of the early '60s, girls in those days could become surfers with nothing more than a bottle of peroxide and an oversized Bing Surfboards T-shirt. Joey Hamasaki, Linda Spheris and Didi Aravelos were great surfers and major exceptions. I also recall Lenny Fox, Crazy Kate and a girl called Kahunk. The surf magazines ran photos of Joyce Hoffman, but few other women.

In 1970, I left LA and migrated to Encinitas where I met one of the best female surfers of the modern era, Margo Godfrey. Margo had moved into a tent in Cheer Critchlow's Cardiff front yard. Occasionally, she and I traveled for waves in her Rambler American, and sometimes we ran into stellar women surfers like Debbie Melville and Jericho Poplar. In Hawaii, Rell Sunn and Lynne Boyer dominated. Slowly, women pulled themselves up from their beach towels and paddled out into the water. Then came the big boom of the '90s. Exclusively women's surf clubs, clothing companies, surf schools, surf camps, magazines, and videos became commonplace. Girl Power flexed hard, and the male establishment backed the project. It wasn't long before women were riding bigger waves and traveling to find surf. At the dawn of the new millennium, an estimated 15 percent of all surfers were women, a greater number than ever before. Or so I thought.

Recently, while rereading Ben Finney's classic: *Surfing, A History of The Ancient Hawaiian Sport*, I recognized my error. Reliable sources quoted by Finney indicate that women in ancient times surfed in equal numbers to men, and with equal skill. These numbers fell off dramatically when surfing was reintroduced to the world in the late 1800s as a Western sport, rather than a Polynesian one. The "new" sport catered to new world attitudes, where a woman's place was in the kitchen, the bedroom, and when everyone was fed, the ironing done and the house spotless, reclining beneath an umbrella, in the sand, waiting for her man to return from the sea. These notions helped to determine who felt comfortable in the water and who did not. More than a century after surfing's rebirth, lyrics from *The Beach Boy's, Surfer Girl*, "...I have watched you on the shore..." proved that little social progress had been made in women's surfing.

In what could be described as a renaissance in women's surfing, there are now signs of life everywhere from Brazil to Washington State, where the Sea Hags spent their reckless youth running on empty and living in old cars in order to surf the frigid Pacific Northwest.

The first story in this book, Kelea's Gift, is based on a woman who would have embraced the Hags as sisters. This Hawaiian princess gave up everything in order to surf. While Kelea ruled the waves 500 years ago, women's surfing is probably much older than that—no doubt as old as the sport itself. Kelea's gift came through her, but it is not from her. Nor is it just for women. Surfing is a gift offered by a creative God, to anyone willing to try it. And, while each of us needs to learn respect, it is up to the elders in the sport to teach it by example. Surfing is inexpensive, but it is not free. Every wave rider owes an unpayable debt to the sea. It is our duty and privilege to clean up the beach. Give a wave or two away. (They never did belong to you anyway). "Hoot a kook," as the great Skip Frye is fond of saying. Save someone from boredom. Maybe, even save a life. As crowds increase we must remember that the fight is not between longboarders, shortboarders, bodysurfers and bodyboarders. It is against those who threaten surfing's very survival with pollution. We must stand firm against them, while keeping open arms to all surfers regardless of creed, color or gender. Only then will surfing's promise be fulfilled and the full measure of Kelea's Gift rain down upon us all.

KELEA'S GIFT

Native legends abound with the exploits of those who attained distinction among their fellows by their skill and daring in this sport (surfing) indulged in alike by both sexes, and frequency too—as in these days of intellectual development—the gentler sex carried off the highest honors.
  —Thrum's Hawaiian Annual 1896

The fishing had been poor, and the surf had been flat for several days. Now the *ali'i* on the Island of Maui were concerned that *Lono* might be angry. Hoping to appease both gods and royalty, many from Lahaina set out before dawn for the *heiau*, armed with sacrificial gifts. As the sun rose, the congregation moved toward the beach, swinging morning glory vines above their heads. Once at the water's edge, they lashed the ocean's surface with the vines, as over one hundred voices chanted in unison:

Ku mai! Ka nalu nui mai Kahiki mai, Alo po'i 'pu! Ku mai ka po huehue, Hu! Kaiko'o loa.
Arise! Ye great surfs from Kahiki, The powerful curling waves. Arise with pohuehue. Well up, long raging surf.

By midday, Princess Kelea was far offshore, paddling her canoe in the calm waters with her brother, Maui's ruling chief, and an attending party, when the south swells began to increase in size. The waves greatly excited Kelea, and by the time she was near shore she could see whitewater on the reefs. The crew paddled harder, catching a wave in the reef pass, and riding it into the lagoon. The waves were big and evenly stacked, and Kelea wished to ride her smaller, more maneuverable *alaia* board. A warm, offshore breeze came off the mountains of her island paradise. She could have ordered anyone to carry her board to the water's edge, but she preferred to do that herself. The small board, which was made from the breadfruit tree, was lighter than most others on Maui, and she manipulated it, not with iron will, but a graceful precision that quickly brought her to the ocean. While some from the royal family hitched rides to the lineup in canoes, Kelea enjoyed paddling in the clear water. Colorful fish moved as one into the dark depths as she stroked. A small reef shark tracked her path into the peak before being rebuked by the royal hand. A much larger tiger shark was menacing the lineup, and the mass of surfers began shouting and beating the water until it too swam away.

The first wave jumped to four feet. Seeing that Kelea was in position to catch it, all riders backed away to watch, fearful lest the penalty of death be applied to the shoulder hopper. She paddled hard, her long, black hair blowing straight back in response to the orchid scented offshore winds. Then she was up, standing tall, smiling, laughing as she surveyed her kingdom. Kelea rode for several hours, and all marveled at her grace and beauty, royals and subjects alike acknowledging her as the best surfer on the island. Back on shore she was given fish, star apples and breadfruit. She ate quietly, watching a strange sight—two outrigger canoes rising on the waves and then disappearing into the trough beyond the reef. She was not familiar with the paddlers or their vessels. They had come from another island, perhaps Oahu. But they were not here for war, there were only two canoes, containing four paddlers each. One of her servant girls began running to call the warriors, but the princess restrained her, not wishing harm on the visitors. The first canoe caught a wave and rode easily into the lagoon. The second canoe was close behind. Even from where she reclined on the soft mat of grass surrounded by the tall swaying palms, Kelea could see that the steersman of the first boat was strong and handsome.

On the beach, the paddlers approached Kelea and her party. They presented gifts of shells, carved bowls, dried fish and octopus. The steersman of the first canoe introduced himself as Kalamakua, a chief from the neighboring island of Oahu.

Kelea nibbled at the food and invited the men to be seated. She wanted to see the canoes that had come from Oahu. They were longer and narrower. "Faster?" the princess wondered aloud. Kalamukua asked if the princess wanted to ride in the canoe. In spite of the warnings of her attendants, she accepted. Once beyond the lagoon a sudden wind squall blew the craft further offshore. Noticing that the second canoe had also left the lagoon, Kelea demanded to be returned to land. There was no answer as the men turned away from Maui and paddled in the direction of their home, Oahu. By the time a party of 20 Maui war canoes had been dispatched to follow the princess and her abductors, the foreigners were only a distant speck. The Oahu canoes proved superior and the distance quickly grew, until the paddlers from Oahu were out of sight. Kelea's heart sank when she realized that she would never again see her beloved home.

The waves pushing through the channel on the 150 mile journey to Oahu were immense, and there was fear expressed by some that they would never again see land. Kelea, who had despaired of her life since realizing her abduction, did not care that the passage was treacherous. Two days and nights passed before the wind died. In that time, the princess had learned to admire Kalamakua's great skill as a paddler, and a powerful, but gentle leader. By the third day, the princess was glad that it was he who had abducted her. But love was *kapu* for this couple. Kalamukua now revealed the full extent of the evil plan, to abduct Kelea, the most beautiful woman and the greatest surf rider of the island, and bring her to the high chief, Lolale, as his wife. Kelea helped with the paddling, and Kalamakua kept his feelings of increasing love and admiration for her inside. As they approached shore, Kelea noticed reefs with good surf, surrounding Oahu.

The canoes made land and were greeted by a party of men, who bowed low to the princess, avoiding her shadow and laying down cloaks for her to walk upon. As she was escorted by royal carriage to the chief, Kelea again noticed the waves. She might enjoy her stay here, after all. But the ride to the chief's quarters broke her heart, moving up into the mountains, far inland, beyond the surf. Lolale was not an evil man as she had imagined, but someone of good of spirit, and while Kelea did not love him, she resigned herself to live with him in her new home.

The princess did not see the ocean for several years, but lived as queen of the entire region, bearing two fat and useless sons and one competent and attractive daughter to Lolale. Her duty fulfilled, Kelea revealed to the chief that she would return to the waves. Realizing that her rank gave her that privilege if she desired it, he reluctantly consented. The chant of Lolale has been preserved:

Farewell, my partner of the lowland plains
On the waters of Pohakea
Above Kanehoa
On the dark mountain spur of Maunauna
O Lihue she has gone
Sniff the sweet scent of the grass
The sweet scent of the vines
That are twisted about by Waikoloa
By the winds of Waiopua
My flower
As if a mote were in my eye
The pupil of my eye is troubled
Dimness covers my eyes
Woe is me.

Kelea was transported to Ewa Beach, and there discovered a band of surfers and a fine *olo* board, lying unused. After convincing those on hand of her high position, the *olo* was loaned to the queen. Riding the biggest waves of the day, she once again distinguished herself as the best surfer in the region. Kalamakua, who had become a high chief and now resided nearby, heard the roar of approval as the queen rode wave after wave in royal splendor. He asked a servant about the cheering, and was told that a beautiful woman was surfing the biggest waves, better than any of the men.

"This is Kelea," said Kalamakua, aloud. But his joy was short lived as he recalled that she was the wife of another high chief. Still, Kalamakua could not resist seeing Kelea ride the waves. Never before had he seen anyone at Ewa ride so gracefully, or for so long a time. Kalamakua paddled out to join Kelea, and together they rode for the remainder of the day. Upon hearing from Kelea that she was no longer married to Lolale, Kalamakua allowed years of strong emotion to surface and requested that she become his wife. The ceremony, which was filled with good food and the exchange of many precious gifts, lasted for over a month. Of course, many waves were ridden at the time, but none so well as those of the queen from Maui.

JIM'S POINT

The logging road had nearly vanished into a sinkhole of mud and water. Half the day had been spent sliding forward at two miles an hour—the second half of the day, digging out, after getting stuck up to the axle in mud as thin as strong coffee. There was relief at seeing the dock until they noticed the fourteen foot wooden boat with the rusty ten horsepower motor that was to take them through the "Graveyard of The Pacific," a stretch of coast that had downed numerous steel-belted freighters, into what they hoped would be a surf paradise.

Hour after hour, they crawled up 25 foot waves, the engine sputtering, threatening to quit on them. When the wind would gust, the tops of the waves would be ripped open and send a misty plume another 25 feet into the air. Then they began the long descent back down the other side of the wave, into the dark trough. They repeated this process a thousand times, at each peak wondering if the rickety craft would hold together as Jim Easterbrook, his wife, Jade, their 125 pound malamute, Siwash, and the captain, a mountain man that the local Indians had given a native name, that translated into the word "Danger," trudged toward the inlet. Jade and Jim hadn't seen the sun since they crossed into Oregon a week earlier. Now they were navigating by the sun, or the shadow of the sun, through a thick curtain of fog in some of the Pacific Northwest's most treacherous seas, in a boat not worthy of Lake Placid on a calm day.

To Jim, it seemed nearly as miraculous as the parting of the Red Sea. The wind blew slightly offshore, the sky cleared, and off in the distance, only a quarter mile to the north, was what he had been searching for, what every surfer searches for, a perfect point wave with nobody out.

It couldn't be real. Coming closer, Jim saw the power walls fold deep and crisp and even on the outside point before they bent into a crescent bay and peeled along the cobblestone point like Malibu, like Rincon, like J-Bay, like nothing he had ever seen. Jim and the captain slipped quickly over the side, and were soon racing double overhead ruler edged bands of energy through sections that demanded full attention and full speed, before being let loose in the inside playground, where they turned and cutback endlessly, riding for four hours, until the need for rest and warmth called them back to the boat. Once on deck again, they decided to make land, and seek accommodations for the night.

The night was black and filled with stars and the friendly and unfriendly sounds of the forest—trees cracking and swaying, birds calling, bears rummaging, raccoons stealing. An hour later there were no sounds but those of wind and the steady, mind-numbing northwestern drip. The little band arose and searched for shelter, that they found beneath a cathedral of tall trees, huddled up around a roaring fire that Jade had somehow managed to start in spite of wet wood and damp matches. The flame served to warm them and keep the bears away. The next morning saw a return of typical weather patterns for the region—drizzle so thick you could drown in it, stiff onshore winds. Fog. The captain sought the Indian chief and his son, two of the only permanent residents of the area, and the hereditary rulers of this vast land. The men had come to respect the captain, but wanted nothing to do with his guests, harboring a rational suspicion and fear of Whites that went back many generations, to the wars of their ancestors. The chief told the captain to return his crew home as soon as the storm passed.

The weather continued to deteriorate, until there was no place left to hide from the wind and rain. The captain bartered away a bottle of tequila to the chief for a broken down shack with no door and a partially collapsed roof. By nightfall, the wind had increased to 90 miles an hour and the rain was falling at an inch an hour. The surf was ripping through the bay, churning top to bottom at 15 feet.

Everyone and everything was wet and cold, but they were safe by Jade's fire, ready to bed down for the night when the chief's son came sliding through the mud, toward them. "Your boat," was all he said, performing his duty before returning from whence he came. The captain tore off his pants and ran, naked, into the storm, followed by Jim, who kept his clothes on. The pair swam into the bay and struggled against the harsh current to bring the boat back to shore. Once there, they tied the boat down to a tree, and returned to the cabin to find yet another problem brewing. The savage scents and sounds of the forest were sending Siwash back to primitive roots, and he would sit up all night, ears perked, lusting for a return to wildness. The dog snarled at the captain, apparently challenging his leadership, snapping twice before grabbing hold and biting completely through his forearm, tearing at it until it was a hunk of bloody meat. With Jim and Jade's help, the captain sewed himself up, and slept with one eye open, while the couple kept their dog at bay. The mountain man and the local Indians wanted to put the dog down, a decision that was postponed until Jim and Jade return to the States, and hired a professional to handle the job.

The next four days were nearly identical as their world shrunk beneath an endless shroud of rain and bitter cold, where nothing, not even sleeping bags or matches remained dry enough for use. The need for warmth and hot food intensified by the hour. The monotony was broken by the appearance of the chief's son at the doorway, saying that his father had declared the waterway safe for travel. To the untrained eye, nothing had changed—the wind howled and the rain fell in sheets. A quick glance at the confused sea made the boy's statement seem like madness. Still, the captain agreed with the chief's assessment. Within an hour, everyone was packed and loaded into the boat, when the chief and his son requested to go along for the ride. The extra weight, that left the boat with only about six inches of freeboard, nearly sank them even before they had cast off.

The chief truly did understand the treacherous waters in this area, and the ride home went smoothly and without incident. The entire party was warmed by the sight of the distant lights of the small town glimmering before them. That's when the little engine finally quit, and the passengers rowed for their lives as the turning tide threatened to flush them back into open ocean, this time without an engine. Three muscle straining hours later, they were at the dock, safe and warm, and ordering refills of hot coffee.

Jim tells the story of his fickle point break often, eyes bright, being sure to keep the location of the spot a secret, hoping to return there someday in the near future, to ride those perfect waves again, even if only for a few blissful hours.

```
          !
        !!!
       !!!!
      !!!!!!
     !!!!!!!!!
    !!!!!!!!!!!
   !!!!!!!!!!!!!
  !!!!!!!!!!!!!!!!
 !!!!!!!!!!!!!!!!!!
!!!!!!!!!!!!!!!!!!!!
!!!!!!!!!!!!!!!!!!!!!
```

DON'T BETRAY

SECRET

SURF SPOTS

```
!!!!!!!!!!!!!!!!!!!!!
!!!!!!!!!!!!!!!!!!!!
!!!!!!!!!!!!!!!!!!
 !!!!!!!!!!!!!!!!
  !!!!!!!!!!!!!
   !!!!!!!!!!!
    !!!!!!!!!
     !!!!!!
      !!!!
       !!!
        !
```

SAIPAN KARAOKE

Discovering surf in the '60s was a matter of pointing your car north or south and driving until you were all alone on some unpaved road that went to an empty beach. It was in this manner that my surf partner, Zero, and I first went to Baja from San Diego on four bald tires without a spare, driving the narrow grave marked mountain roads, barreling through Ensenada, turning toward the coast and rolling out until we found a beach where we slept for the night and awoke to waves and two fishermen rowing in a big hammerhead shark, taking up the length of their panga. Going north was no less of an adventure, crossing the Golden Gate Bridge, through miles of winding roads until we found the coast and rough, cold waves breaking in some rocky cove. After that it was Hawaii, and then the island of Guam.

Guam was home base and we worked in the hotels as gardeners by day and waiters by night, saving money for further exploration of the Mariana Island chain. We had heard of a neighboring island, Saipan, which was accessible by plane because the Japanese had done such a splendid job of building small airports all over that section of the Pacific during the War. Upon arrival in Saipan, Zero and I found signs of life and headed for the one little hotel, and laid our sleeping bags, backpacks and surfboards out just beyond it, in a coconut grove where the loose coconuts fell all around us like cannonballs. We found a tree with green coconuts and camped beneath it, unaware that coconut crabs were everywhere, ready to pinch off a finger with a grip that we later heard was strong enough to snap a screwdriver in two.

The night passed, as it often does in uncertain surroundings, in sleep that feels more like a trance, jerking awake once, after dreaming that a tidal wave was hitting the island. Then there were the mosquitoes, so plentiful that we gave up trying to kill them, donating blood as they penetrated every available pore until dawn, when we awoke to micro surf peeling over a shallow reef. The water was warm, and we were on the lookout for stonefish and as-sorted other deadly sea creatures.

Surveying our surroundings from our surfboards the potential for waves looked good, but we could see that it would take one of Saipan's famous typhoons to blow through and make it great. That night Zero prayed for a typhoon to hit, the irony that a typhoon would level the island in the name of God, completely escaping him.

The next morning the surf was completely flat, and Zero climbed a coconut tree, and we had green spoon meat coconut and milk, nourishing stuff that lacks the cannonball effect that an American breakfast offers to the internal organs. We dressed and walked to the hotel. It was a nice two-story, Spanish styled place with wrought iron terraces, a pool and a black tie waiter serving customers, mostly military personnel who had come over from Guam. The waiter spoke decent Filipino-influenced English, and we had eggs, rice, Spam and papaya. At the next table a woman sat alone—mid 20s, not unattractive, drinking something with a tiny paper umbrella in it, lifting her glass occasionally to Zero. She had that deadly mid-Western combination of white skin and big blonde on brunette hair. Zero guessed correctly at Omaha and earned himself a Harvey Wallbanger. Clever conversation earned him another and another.

Her name was Peggy, and she had come to Saipan with her husband, a Green Beret who knew over six ways to kill us both in less than seven seconds, she said. Feeling the effects of the alcohol, Zero laughed. Feeling the effects of the Spam, I excused myself. When I returned, Zero and Peggy were well acquainted, and the table was two glasses deeper with Harvey Wallbangers, that she put on her tab along with our breakfast. Peggy periodically put her hand into Zero's, and laughed and ordered two more Harvey Whatsisnames, a phrase that she found cute enough to repeat two or three more times to the waiter.

Like the good little drunk she was, she would go through the steps—laugher, tears and rage. She had stalled on step two and was telling Zero how the love of her life, a man that she respectfully called the Sergeant, had taken her away from her waitressing career on Guam, to Saipan where the two were married in an ancient Chomoro ceremony, performed by the chef at the hotel. She said the chef was some sort of ancient island priest, and she showed little surprise to find him out of priestly garb, in shorts and slaps, sharing a drink and a smoke with a young woman. She was sure that the Sergeant loved her, and rationalized his leaving without a word on the very night after they had become one flesh, her being a virgin and all before that time, as she said, crying that he had ruined her and that no decent man would want her now. But the Sergeant was a great man, according to her, and there were things that nobody knew, and he was off to fight the communists in some dark jungle some place. He wouldn't be back until the world was free for all men. "I love him. God, really I do." Step three came without warning and a typhoon of ruined dreams hit with lies thicker than wet mascara, and I excused myself and swam in the warm water of the lagoon.

I returned to find Zero seated on a lawn chair by the pool, Peggy's head in his lap, her apparently drifting in and out of consciousness while he gently pressed his hand against her springy hair. Neither Zero nor I had been in the company of women for six or seven months, on the road, chasing surf as we were, and the idea of a girl, especially when he had alcohol running around his brain, warped Zero's already normally poor judgement. "Patty's asked me to stay in Saipan with her," he said. I looked at him in disbelief, a look that he read well. "I can't leave her here like this. Besides, I love her." He paused and then added, "and she loves me." He hadn't had a drink in six months, but he was drunk now, and when he was drinking there was no use arguing. That night we all went to the hotel club, and watched a Filipino man with tight black pants and an unbuttoned white silk shirt do Tom Jones, accompanied by a scratchy record player. "You and your pussycat nose" is even funnier with a Filipino accent. His screeching and strutting was rewarded with tips and the adoration of the bar's patrons, and one pair of women's extra large underwear that floated to the stage floor like a parachute, before he picked them up and put them on his head. The crowd went wild.

I slept on the floor of the hotel room that night. Zero shared the bed with Peggy, who sat up occasionally to take a pint bottle from under her pillow, and drink rum straight from the bottle while Zero snored loudly and I contemplated going back to the mosquitoes before hard rain ruined things.

The morning was filled with the usual drunken shame and silent apologies, him backing off, her moving forward. They tried to care about something other than their own emotional survival. Then came artificial kisses on his part, and sobbing on her part as we said goodbye, packed quickly and took the plane in 45 minutes of silence back to Guam.

It didn't take a week of female deprivation before Zero found the Cherry Moon Bar, got drunk, and took the night plane to Saipan. He called the next morning, drunk and happy to say that a swell was hitting the reefs in front of the hotel, and that I should hurry up and get over there to surf and be the best man in his wedding. I took the next plane out.

The Saipan morning was filled with small waves, only Zero and I out, sharp coral and a broken fin sending me to the beach before starvation did. She was waiting poolside for us, and she ordered breakfast and drinks all around. When we passed on the drinks, she ordered breakfast for Zero and said that she would drink for all of us, which she did. It was the same old three step elevator drop into hell that always ended in rage's basement, this time almost justified since she had over $2,000 on her bill that we had helped to run up and would we be so kind as to... Two thousand dollars equaled a lot of Wallbangers and eggs, and Zero, sober for the first time in days, escaped with me to the airport.

Then came the late night calls, friendly laughter, pleading, crying and rage, in that order. The calls stopped suddenly, and it was at least a month before we heard from her again, this time asking for us to come and hear her sing. She was paying off her hotel bill, replacing the Filipino, doing a one-woman act of Andrew's Sisters tunes. I said that I thought it amazing that one woman could do the Andrew's Sisters, but Zero said that she had enough personalities inside of her to do not only the sisters, but both parents, brothers, aunts, uncles and second cousins.

THE METALLIC SEA HORSE

By Rob Morton

Keki was paddling his heavy hollow log canoe the last three miles home, his aching muscles working smoothly. He ran the same word-picture over and over again, in his mind. Evinrude, Evinrude. The name of Doctor Jackson's outboard motor had a powerful effect upon his mind, now almost numb from the grueling paddle home. Evinrude, Evinrude, the name rang through his brain in the same rhythm as his paddle strokes.

Keki's paddle made small, twisting whirlpools of water every time he struck downward and forcefully pulled through each stroke. The disappearing trail of whirlpools followed for a short distance behind Keki's canoe. He began to contrast his ancient method of paddling with the force and magnitude of the mighty Evinrude. The Evinrude, the mighty metallic sea horse, churning up an endless white wake through the dark blue sea. Doctor Jackson must be a chief among his own people thought Keki. Only a warrior of great renown could own such a creature as the metallic sea horse. Evinrude, Evinrude, the mantra continued in the same rhythm as his paddle strokes.

Doctor Jackson was sensitive to the shock his arrival would bring to one of the last of the long isolated Pacific island cultures. He hoped, as did his fellow Methodist missionaries, that they could soften the blow of advancing civilization. The Methodist Church had already established a mission of proven benefit a day's journey away. Doctor Jackson's arrival among Keki's people was in advance of a new mission planned for them.

In these post-war years, missionaries were better educated than their forebears, they had learned the lessons of Hawaii. In 19th century Hawaii, missionaries mistakenly broke down traditional values in the islands. Paving the way for the virtual destruction of the Hawaiian people left them open to every vice and disease from Europe and America. Now in the middle of the 20th century, new developments in cultural anthropology had made Christian missionaries sensitive to the ravages of cultural upheaval that the best intended Christians could make upon innocent indigenous people.

Keki was now two miles out and continued his slow, methodical strokes. He looked up in the gathering darkness toward his island, still visible in this twilight hour. Doctor Jackson's Westinghouse high powered electric bulb suddenly flashed on. Powered by a Ford Motor Company generator, it projected a streak of silver light across the darkening water, that ran straight to Keki's canoe.

Keki still felt excitement every time he saw the electric light. He no longer had to put on a brave show in front of the Ford generator, with its mechanical roar. Even the island children danced around it now. And everyone rejoiced at the sight of the Westinghouse light. On this same evening, at the same hour, in the same darkening twilight that was beginning to envelope Keki, Doctor Jackson's wife and children were at home in the suburbs of Sydney, Australia. Sitting in the glow of an American made television, a 19 inch black and white Motorola, they watched the Jackson family favorite, Australian rugby. Doctor Jackson himself had been an outstanding member of the university team.

Doctor Jackson and the missionary council had already discussed introducing organized rugby to the island, hoping that it could act as an alternative rite of passage into manhood, replacing the age old lethal and savage martial arts of inter-island combat still necessary to prove a boy's coming of age.

Sensitive as they were to native cultural values, the missionaries were greatly alarmed at the ancient tradition of old men, retired from battle, expertly handcrafting weapons of war for younger combatants who cheerfully displayed their skill and valor in the spectacular arts of war. In this ancient theater, Keki had proven to be an accomplished player, having several kills to his credit.

Strangely, Doctor Jackson could not repress a secret admiration for Keki and his warrior brethren. Whenever they would practice martial arts with their beautifully crafted weapons, Doctor Jackson would always try to find time to watch them. The obvious athletic skill and grace of their practice would have great appeal for a vigorous man with the doctor's speed and coordination. However, being a worthy Christian, he could only think of meeting Keki on a level playing field of rugby.

Keki was now finishing his long paddle home. The long, monotonous paddle strokes were coming to an end for the evening. Returning from the outlying reefs, dangerously populated with black tipped reef sharks, his canoe was heavily loaded with large fish. It was on these trips that young men of the island displayed another form of athletic prowess. Spear fishing for the tribe, many young men had lost limbs to the black tipped sharks.

One last thrust of the paddle, and the heavy log canoe slid silently up onto the soft white sand. With a shout to announce his arrival, Keki waited for the young boys and women to rush down and help him unload his catch. When this was done, Keki joined a group of spectators who had gathered to watch Doctor Jackson perform surgery at his open-sided workstation. Doctor Jackson rarely noticed the circle of faces that gathered nightly at the edge of the light. The circle of light thrown out by the Westinghouse bulb seemed to create an artificial barrier, separating island spectators from Doctor Jackson while the mild roar of the generator announced the arrival of the 20th century.

Keki sat in wide-eyed admiration of Doctor Jackson, who began the first in a series of surgical incisions to straighten a child's cleft lip. What a strange and wonderful man, thought Keki. A white man has left his own world to travel so far with these metallic machines and give us the miracles of his knowledge. Keki instinctively noticed the doctor's lean, athletic build and natural grace, concluding that he must be a fine warrior. I will teach him the art of our warfare, and he will teach me his, thought Keki, generously.

Still seated at the barrier's edge of the Westinghouse light, Keki's mind began to wander. He stared past Doctor Jackson to the Evinrude outboard motor propped up against a nearby tree. He began to have visions of the mighty metallic sea horse, which made his pulse quicken. He pictured the metallic sea horse catching small rainbows in its spray. He saw the billowing spray arching high over the endless churning white wake, that lit up the dark blue sea. He could hear the unearthly power of the motor's roar. It made his palms sweat. Only the fallen ancient warriors in the next world have ridden such a magical creature. Keki could feel the ancient ones looking down at him from the next world, expectantly. Adrenaline coursed through his veins.

A month later, three Methodist missionaries arrived on the island, two men and one young woman. Doctor Jackson had failed to report to his mission or return for fresh supplies. In a long skiff, powered by an 80 HP outboard motor, the Christian missionaries slid up onto the same soft white sand that Keki's canoe had slid onto one month earlier. The arrival of an Evinrude 80 HP outboard motor produced the same response as the original Evinrude outboard motor had, when it first appeared on Doctor Jackson's boat. In this relatively short span, the islanders had not shown that universal capacity of mankind, to grow jaded with new technology overnight.

The missionaries were warmly received by the islanders, who rushed down to greet them. They thanked the missionaries for coming in peace, and not bearing arms, which was taken as a sign of courtesy, in these islands.

The new arrivals were taken to Doctor Jackson's workstation, which was strangely decorated with long and plentiful garlands of flowers. A spent ring of black torches circled the station, which obviously had been used in a ceremony. One large, brightly painted death mask hung over the doorway. At this strange sight, the young Miss

Wellington began crying. Mister Owens and Mister Hopkins were suddenly stricken with nausea. The islanders cheerfully told the missionaries how they had given Doctor Jackson's corpse a splendid death ceremony, to free his soul from this world. He now lived with the ancient ones, in the next world, an honor for any warrior. He will never be forgotten on this island, the missionaries were informed. His death mask will have a place of honor in our communal house, beside other fallen chiefs.

Keki now emerged from his thatched house. The first and original Evinrude 80 HP outboard motor ever seen on the island lay outside of his door. The missionaries reacted with horror as he approached, for he was wearing the bright red insignia cap of Doctor Jackson's university rugby club.

ONE SURFER WRITES

Dear Chris,
I am Woodbridge Parker Brown. I was born on January 5, 1912 in New York City. As a child I always wanted to fly, but found I didn't want power planes. I wanted to fly with nature, where my head was my motor (like the birds).

I married an English girl and we went to La Jolla, California, where I flew gliders (sailplanes) at Torrey Pines. We would tow off the beach with a car, up into the updraft, where we could stay up all day.

During this time, I would bodysurf on the beach. One day I found a piece of wood on the beach and put it under me as I rode the waves. I found that this helped, so I bought a plank of wood, and shaped it like a fish, with a pointed tail. This was a great improvement, and allowed me to stay a little ahead of the whitewater, and slide a little left or right. But I had to start only as far out as I could push off of the bottom. As I looked out at the biggest waves curling outside, I thought I could build a hollow board that would hold me up. I could catch them outside, before they broke, and the waves said to me, "Yes, I will let you slide across my face, and we can both enjoy it." So I did! The board was eight feet long, twenty-three inches wide, four inches thick, and weighed twelve pounds. It worked fine.

The trouble with flying at Torrey Pines was that when the big storms would come in and give us our best flying conditions, it also made the tides, and big waves that covered the beach, so the car could not go. So I thought, I will take off at the top edge of the cliff, like the Germans do, with a shock cord. Three rubber bands one inch thick, and 50 feet long, attached to a rope going through a dead man's pulley, then to the car. As the car takes off, it stretches out the rubber shock cord, and zips the glider off the edge of the cliff. But this was a dangerous operation, because if anything happened, there was no room to stop the glider.

One day after a big storm the car took off, but the wheels were spinning in the mud, getting little traction. As

I started toward the cliff edge, I realized that I didn't have enough speed, so I ground looped, that is I dug one wing tip into the ground, and spun myself around, with the back half of the glider sticking out over the edge of the cliff! So we decided that this was not a safe operation.

We finally figured out that if we tied one end of the rope to a stake in the ground, then to a pulley on the car, then to the glider way back from the edge of the cliff, the glider would be going twice the speed of the car, giving enough time and altitude to recover from any trouble. This worked fine.

The day after I made a world distance record with my glider, my wife died, and I cracked up mentally. I never flew again, just walked the streets all night—I couldn't sleep. So, I started to bum around the world, and ended up in Waikiki Beach in Hawaii. But I kept on surfing, and I really feel that surfing kept me alive.   I was so despondent and down, I would stay out on my surfboard all day and when night came, I was so exhausted I could get a little sleep.

Finally, I found a part Hawaiian girl, and had two beautiful children. I built the first catamaran, and brought it on the beach to give the tourists a thrill ride on the fastest sailboat in the world. And they loved it, and I made my living from that. But my wife died, and I was left alone again. But now I am married again, and I have a twelve-year old son, and we both go surfing together. If competition comes into it with strife, hate and envy, it is no longer a sport and ceases to be working with nature. I see God in the beauty of nature, those beautiful blue swells in the beautiful glassy smooth water, and the surfer's cry of joy and thrill as he slides across her radiant face!

I used to enjoy surfing with Scooter Boy because he had his dog Sandy with him on the board, and he would run forward and back on the board to hold onto the smallest wave as it came to shore.

God is Love for all.
Love, Woody Brown 5/16/99

MURPH THE SURF

To my left is a mountain of a man with his blue denim shirt unbuttoned, revealing a swastika that makes a ten inch journey down his cut abdomen. Just below the swastika, lining his iron waist, are the words: White Power. To my right are two men of equal stature, Black Muslims, if I can trust my guide and judge by their appearance. They eye White Power and me closely. Two armed-guards pace a catwalk, twenty-some feet above us, but a world away. A sign directly above us reads, "No Warning Shots." If something starts, it won't end without blood.

We are in the maximum-security section of Donovan State Prison, and these men, along with 500 others who have been convicted of violent crimes, have gathered to hear America's most famous jewel thief, Jack "Murph the Surf" Murphy, speak about his fast times.

I am here because of a call from the world famous surfer, David Nuuhiwa, who is also visiting inmates as Murph's guest, and part of Bill Glass' Weekend of Champions, a group that attempts to bring the light of the gospel into our national hellholes, on an almost weekly basis. Earlier, Tino Wallenda, a key member of the world's most famous high-wire family, had revealed how his father fell over 100 feet, to his death. Later that afternoon, Wallenda will walk the wire for the prisoners, lecturing them about their own mortality, as he tiptoes with death, shielded from eternity by nothing but a quarter inch cable. The act will get the attention of men who have risked their lives for other reasons—anger, revenge, drugs, money. The words of Sandi Fatow, who once traveled with Jimi Hendrix, became involved with the Miami underworld and hit bottom as a Harlem junkie before making the same U-turn that Murphy and his band of gypsies have taken, seem to penetrate. All of the storytellers have one thing in common—they have damaged their lives and found redemption through Jesus Christ, who pulled them out of their own private hells.

But it's Murphy who the men are here to see—hoping

to hear the stories of prison riots, running mega scams and pulling the biggest jewel heist in history. They will get more than they bargained for.

Sixty-two year old Jack Roland Murphy bounces onto the stage like a teenaged inmate jacked on meth. I know a little about his early days—how he grew up in Carlsbad, California in the '50 with famed surfers L.J. Richards and Phil Edwards, before moving to Pittsburgh, to become such a brilliant violinist that he was offered a chair with their Philharmonic Orchestra, even before he graduated high school. His athleticism earned him a tennis scholarship at the University of Pittsburgh, and eventually a gig as an acrobatic and high tower diver with Barnum and Bailey Circus. But the boy wanted to surf again, and the Pittsburgh winters drove him south to Florida, where he discovered warm water and good waves at places like Sebastian Inlet. Within a few years he was considered the East Coast's top surfer, winning the state championships in the early '60. But Miami held other attractions for a smart, athletic kid. There was easy money to be made.

One night Murph and an accomplice made their way to New York City, to the back lot of the New York Museum of Natural History. Patiently waiting for the guards to make their rounds, they climbed over a steel spiked fence that dropped down into a sunken courtyard next to a large dark building. Scaling several chain-linked fences until they reached the 125-foot wall, they climbed, cautiously, maneuvering their way up to a narrow ledge that wrapped itself around the building, five floors up. Just as planned, they were directly over the J.P. Morgan gem room. They entered the research lab on the top floor through an unlocked window where Murph secured the end of the 125-foot rope, which he carried with him. He lowered the line into the gem room, and the pair silently cascaded to their destination.

The next five hours were a joyous romp in the park for Murph and his partner. By early morning, the cat burglars had lifted the Midnight Sapphire, the largest black sapphire in the world; the DeLong Ruby, the world's most perfect star ruby; the Eagle Diamond, the largest diamond ever found in America and 23 other precious gems, including the ultimate prize, the Star of India, the largest star sapphire in the world, with a mysterious 300 year history, from their reinforced cases. That night, Murph and his partner celebrated at the Metropolitan Jazz Lounge in Times Square where legendary drummer, Gene Krupa, was performing with his band. Nudging the drummer, Murph quipped, "Krupa, you'd never guess what I've got in my pocket." They rolled down to Greenwich Village with Krupa and his crowd, where they sat with Herbie Mann for a jazz session at the Village Gate.

Thugs, thieves, rapists and murderers are dead silent. Murph the Surf is a big prison celebrity who they respect, just as their predecessors respected another of Chaplain Ray's men, George Meyer, The Devil's Driver, a penitent gangster who wheeled the getaway car for Capone during the Saint Valentine's Day Massacre. Having served over two decades in similar joints, Murphy understands the volatile nature of the men before him, and yet he shows no fear of them. "You think you're tough. You're not tough," he begins. I'm looking for a safe exit. There are none. The Nazi's jaw tightens. Others assume threatening postures, as if to prove Murph wrong. To illustrate true toughness, Jack tells the story of a man who was nailed to a cross and never made a sound. He tells them how the man took the rap for them. Of course there's the story of his big jewel heist and subsequent three-year confinement. Within one year he's in prison again, this time for a long stretch that multiplies when he leads a massive prison riot. By the time Murph's rebellion has been spent, he's looking at double life, plus 20 years. The story of his parole is miraculous. The outlaw portion of his life is turned into a popular movie and proves the inspiration for television's jewel heist genre. What Murphy considers the real story, however, his conversion, has largely been left undocumented by mainstream media.

The show is over, and I relax along with the Nazi's facial muscles. The Muslims, who have listened politely, leave quietly. Most of the men drift numbly back to reading books or writing letters in their bunks. Some stick around. A man convicted of killing his wife tells a counselor, "I haven't cried in 25 years, and now I can't stop." Another man asks some difficult questions concerning the fairness of God. The team prays with him and dozens of others. Some men unsuccessfully hold back tears as they read Bible passages first heard a lifetime ago, in a child's Sunday school class.

An inmate asks Murphy, "What are you doing here? When I get out I'm never coming back." Murph replies, "I'm an expert on doing time. I served over 21 years. Since then I've been to over 1,200 different prisons, and I've found that it doesn't matter if you're behind bars or not. If you're not doing God's business, you're still just doing time."

These days find Jack Murphy on the road with a gang of some of the baddest criminals that this country has ever confined. They are joined by the same types of pimps, prostitutes, hustlers and gangsters that Jesus Christ embraced 2,000 years earlier. Also on the roster there are NFL stars, a world-class ventriloquist and a biker gang. The Champion's show has changed countless lives across America, Puerto Rico and Mexico. Thousands enjoy freedom because of the experience that Murph the Surf calls "The most exciting thing I've ever done in my life." Coming from him, that's saying something.

SARAH

I first noticed her in the park, where she was catching tadpoles, and carefully putting them into a little glass goldfish aquarium. The year was 1960. I was 12 and she was 13, tall and blonde, with braids and freckles. Cute as Sandra Dee. The next day I saw her again, and she asked me to play catch with her. Then I discovered that she could throw a curveball that broke almost a foot before landing right over the plate, nearly every time. From then on Sarah was my best friend. She was a better kickball player than any of. us boys were. She could climb a tree faster than a monkey, running up the limbs to the tree house that my father had built for the neighborhood kids in our backyard, beating everyone else to the top whenever we had meetings there.

I loved going to her house. She had a tipi in her backyard. Next to it were cages that she had built by hand, out of glass and wood. The cages were filled with snakes, lizards and horned toads, which she called by the Latin name, *insectivorous iguanid lizards*. Other cages were filled with bugs and frogs and baby birds. There was an incubator fashioned from a cardboard box and a light bulb where she kept abandoned birds alive by feeding them with eyedroppers of mashed up food. Like every other boy, I was secretly in love with her.

She had grown up in Huntington Beach before her parents were killed in a car accident and she was called inland to live with her uncle and aunt. She was the first girl surfer that I had ever known. We planned to meet at my house Saturday morning, and then hitchhike to Huntington, and go surfing and wander the hills there for reptiles. She said that we could sleep in her grandmother's attic, a woman who was not really her grandmother, but an old woman that Sarah helped out by mowing her lawn and weeding her grass and doing other chores. I told my parents that I was going to spend the weekend in her tipi, and she told her guardians that she was going to stay with a girlfriend. There were not many ways to get into trouble in those days, and so nobody checked on our stories.

At exactly five that Saturday morning, Sarah came bouncing down the white line of the street on her pogo stick, braids flying. You could see her all over town, bouncing through the city streets, bouncing to the library, bouncing through the shopping center, and even bouncing to and from school, when it was in session. Now, she bounced up onto the sidewalk and followed the cement path, to the porch where I was seated, waiting for her. She jumped from the stick, and her big moccasin-covered feet landed on the ground, right next to me. She gave a curtsey, and laid the stick in the ivy of our front yard.

I had packed two lunches and filled my father's army canteen with Kool-Aid. In my pocket were three quarters, stolen from Mother's purse, just in case. Then we walked to the boulevard and waited at the side of the road, where Sarah collected cigarette butts and stuffed the tobacco into a corncob pipe that we smoked. Hitchhiking was easy, but we sometimes got rides from men who drove fast and wanted to touch me or her, or women with fancy cars and fake jewelry who were kind and bought us lunch, served with a lecture about the dangers of hitchhiking. Often we got rides in the back of pickup trucks, telling dirty jokes and laughing until we were let out to wait for our next ride.

In Huntington, we found Grandmother's old wooden house, all white, ivy covered shingles, surrounded by a large lawn with pink flowers, neat in their beds, and several old dusty oak trees. Grandmother met us on the porch, kissed each of us on the cheek and pointed the way to the musty attic, where we would be comfortable, sleeping on army cots.

At the beach, all the surfers knew Sarah, and it was no trouble borrowing light fiberglass surfboards. Watching surfers like Sarah and some of her friends like U.S. surfing champion, Jack Haley, made me realize that I was not a good surfer. I had surfed a few times with my father, and was good enough to catch a wave and ride at an angle, but Sarah could turn, walk the nose and shoot the pier.

The surf was only three to four feet, and I watched from behind as she rode tall through the pilings and came out on the other side. When I tried, I became scared half way, lost my balance and came up from the soup just in time to see the borrowed board hit the pier. There was a big ding in the board and I paddled in. Not seeing the board's owner, I bit into a bar of paraffin wax, chewed it, filled the ding with it as best I could, covered the board with sand, and left it on the beach.

About a half an hour later, Sarah found me on the pier. I was using a trick that a friend had taught me, to approach old women and say that my father had run out of gas and that we needed a nickel or a dime in order to get home. They always felt sorry for you, and usually gave you a buck or two. I had six or seven bucks, more than enough for Sarah and I to eat at the Buzz Inn, across from the pier. Back at Grandma's house, we sat in the attic, surveying her home-drawn map of the hills in the area. She had a navy surplus backpack and a pair of binoculars that her father had lifted from a dead Nazi during the War. She put the binoculars into the pack, along with my canteen and the sack lunches that I had made. She gave me a hunting knife in a leather sheaf, and said that I could keep it. I strapped it onto my belt, and practiced my quick-draw. She went into the garage and returned with a bow and a quiver of arrows, stuffed into the cardboard sheaf that she had made. She handed them to me, and I slung the bow and arrows over my shoulder.

It was a good sunny day as we hiked up the grade, to the dirt path that led into the hills. The path was loaded with rabbits that sprang out from beneath our feet as we walked and I shot wildly at them, missing each time as they sprang into bushes or holes where we did not see them again. Looking through the binoculars, Sarah always spotted the rabbits before I did. Then, she would whisper, "Stop." I would freeze in my tracks and she would hand me the binoculars, making the rabbit look as big as a big dog, even from far away. We would move slowly, on tiptoes, to where the rabbit was sitting. I would shoot, but miss every time.

Owls, hawks, pheasants and mud hens were the targets of my arrows, but I never landed any of them. I did shoot an owl square in the chest once, but the shot was weak, and my arrow bounced off, scattering feathers everywhere before it flew away. I caught a horned toad with my hand, and put it into the shoebox that Sarah was carrying. She had punched holes into the roof of the box, and stuffed it with leaves and grass to keep the horned toad and any other animals that we caught, alive until she could put them into their cages. She caught a tree frog and a small garter snake, which I was afraid to touch at first, thinking that it was a rattler. When I saw that the snake was harmless, I held it nervously in my hand. Sarah tried to force the frog into the snake's mouth, but the snake kept squirming out of my hand, falling to the ground and slithering in the dust. Then I would have to catch it again, even though I was still a little scared of it. She let both the frog and the snake go free in the bushes by a little pond of muddy water where a million tadpoles were swimming, some of them sprouting tiny new legs, half way to becoming frogs. We left the shoebox with the horned toad hidden behind a tumbleweed, near the pond.

As I wandered from the path, a little cottontail darted off from under my feet. I shot and barely missed, and it ran away into the cactus patch before I could get another arrow out of the sheaf. There was no place for the rabbit to hide, and I ran after it, as fast as I could, keeping an arrow tight against the string. I found the rabbit with its back to me, on a small grassy mound, a few feet beyond the cactus patch. It was eating grass with its head down, quietly, unaware that I was pointing an arrow at its heart. The arrow flew fast and straight, running through the rabbit's back, and coming out in the gut, pinning it to the ground. It squirmed on the dirt, twisting and turning, trying to break free from the shaft. I ran up closer and shot again, hitting it high on the back this time.

Sarah ran up the hill after me, breathing hard and laughing. She offered to finish off the little rabbit with her knife, saying that we could eat the meat, and use the fur to make moccasins. I had another arrow pulled, ready to kill the rabbit myself, who was still jerking around, trying to break free from my arrows. Then I saw that it was just a baby cottontail, and that the snow-white fur was turning red from blood. When it turned its little pink eyes to me, I started crying. Sarah bent down and stuck her knife into the rabbit's neck, killing it quickly and sending blood everywhere. She looked back at me sternly, because I had not quit crying.

"If we hurry, we can wash all of the blood out of the fur before it dries," she said happily. "No, I just want to go home," I said through my tears, dropping the bow in the dirt, turning my back on her, embarrassed that a girl had seen me cry. After a little while, I turned to face her again, hoping to achieve her pity. She was sharpening her knife on the whetstone that she pulled from her pocket, and she shrugged her shoulders after lifting her head to look at me. Then she picked up the dead rabbit, put it onto a flat rock, cut out the guts and skinned it. She threw the guts into the cactus patch, wrapped the meat in the wax paper that she took from our sandwiches, and dropped the still quivering flesh into her backpack. The bloodstained fur, she took over to the little creek that ran through the hills and emptied into a pond. She washed the fur clean on a rock as the clear water from the creek ran red. She wiped the knife blade clean of blood and walked over to the cactus patch to lop off a few red cactus apples. She skinned the wild fruit and cut away the fine needles. Sitting down, she ate a cactus apple as if it were a regular apple or an orange bought from the store. She offered me one. It was good and I stopped crying.

We ate our sandwiches and drank all of the Kool-Aid. Then we cleaned our red stained hands in the creek and got up to continue our search for horned toads. She didn't understand why I had cried, but she never said anything about it. "Be bold," I said to myself, repeating words that my grandfather always said to me. We continued to tramp through the hills. If I found another rabbit I would kill it quickly, and skin it myself.

We walked until we came to a large pond, and waded across the cold, shallow water, following the sound of Mexican music to the river where Sarah had seen baby turtles and caught crawdads in a coffee can the last time she was here. A small dam had recently been built upriver, however, and all that we saw now were a few dead turtles and frogs on the riverbank. Sarah said that nothing lived in the river anymore. Still, the water was clear and cold and good to drink. A man and a woman sat together on the sandy banks with their legs in the river. Three young boys wore their pants into the running water, splashed each other and skipped rocks from one bank to the other. The woman was fat and wet, wearing a flower-print dress and a big hat. The man sat with his trousers rolled up and his legs in the water, playing an accordion while the woman sang. She had a pretty Mexican voice, and together they sounded as good as one of my grandfather's records. Sarah showed me how to walk like an Indian, without making a sound. We drank from the stream and filled the canteen without anyone seeing us. Then we hiked up past the place she called rabbit hill, onto the plateau, beyond the grove of palms to a place called the great desert on Sarah's map. Here was sand and nothing grew. We tiptoed over to a place with a few trees that her map called hobo camp.

We hid in the bushes and watched the hobos from a safe distance. There, sitting in a small grove of trees, were three men. They were huddled around a fire, beneath a worn out blanket that was hung up in the tree branches to protect them from the sun. Two of the men sat in the dirt and shade, and one squatted out of the shade, sometimes turning his face directly into the sun. They were ragged and dirty. There were empty tin cans, milk bottles, broken beer bottles and newspapers scattered all over the ground. The shortest of the hobos had curly, blond hair and a blond, scruffy beard. There was a giant hobo with black stubble on his face, and fresh blood over one eye. The third man was tall and skinny and wore a hat pulled down over his face so that I could not tell what sort of man he was. The food they were cooking in an old can smelled pretty good. They were passing a bottle around.

We whispered to each other as we laid low behind the bushes to spy on the hobos. Sarah showed me how to cup my hands around my ears so that I could hear them better. Now we heard everything. I was a little scared and wanted to leave, but she wanted to stay. The little hobo tilted the bottle up to his mouth even after there was nothing in it. Then, he threw the bottle into the fire and we heard it break.

He shouted something about "old Charlie," a friend of theirs who had been sent to jail. The little hobo spoke, making the words stronger by waving his knife in the air, saying that he was going to bust old Charlie out as soon as he had the chance. The big hobo said that they couldn't bust Charlie out because there were too many cops around the jail, and they would be caught. The little hobo shouted that the big hobo was no friend of his or of old Charlie's. Then the big hobo punched the little hobo in the face, and the little hobo dropped the knife he was holding, onto the dirt. He looked for the knife for a moment, and when he could not find it, he came after the big hobo with a flaming branch that he took from the fire. The big hobo kicked the branch out of the little hobo's hand. He got him down and they wrestled on the dirt, rolling in our direction as the big hobo pounded the little hobo's face. They were getting close to our hiding place, and we decided to move on. Even after we had walked a long way, keeping low so that they would not spot us, we could hear the little hobo yelling out that he gave up the fight. By then we had gone up high enough to see them through the binoculars as they drank from a new bottle, punching each other, and screaming at the blue sky.

From time to time, I peaked into the sack to see the pink, greasy meat of the rabbit. We walked for a long time and climbed a steep hill, going through a tangle of trees until we came out onto a patch of thin, yellow dust. Sarah bent down and dug in the dirt with her knife, surprising me when she came up with two petrified clams and one petrified snail. She gave me one of the clams as a present, saying that it proved the story of Noah and the Ark. I was happy to think about God. I caught a horned toad, but Sarah took it from me and turned it loose in the bushes. When I asked why she turned it loose, she rubbed her belly and said that it was pregnant. Then I remembered the girl I had heard about at school who was pregnant. I turned away from Sarah.

We walked over the short new green grass of the hills, holding hands through fields of large yellow flowers as high as our heads, and small purple flowers as high as our waists. When we got back to where the trail began, we picked up the horned toad in the box, and she let that one go also. The sun was setting and turned the dirt and the old junk cars and even the oil wells bright orange and gold. When the mosquitoes came out, we squashed them against our arms and faces, feeling so happy about everything else that we hardly even noticed them. We could hear crickets and bullfrogs and small fish jumping in the pond for the mosquitoes. When we stopped and Sarah kissed me, I hit her in the arm and ran home to Grandmother's house. I arrived before Sarah did, avoiding her by pretending to be asleep in the hammock on the front porch, when she came home.

I never left the hammock, but lay still, watching the stars come out, thinking about Sarah and all the things we had done, awake long into the night. Then I slept hard, not waking again until late the next morning when I saw her walking up the sidewalk, to the house. Her hair was wet, and so I knew that she had been surfing with her friends. Before she saw me, I jumped up, still wearing my clothes from the day before. I pulled the hunting knife from its sheaf and began killing weeds with it. Pretending not to see her as she passed, I watched from the corner of my eye as she entered the house. I worked for about an hour, stopping only to wipe my brow with my sleeve. When she came out to the front yard, she had a greasy paper sack with her, and she knelt down to join me, picking weeds, silently, with a screwdriver. After a while she stopped and I stopped and she told me that the waves at the pier were good, and that we should go out again later. Then she said that Dennis, the guy I had borrowed the board from, was looking for me. "What did you do with his board, Jack?" she asked. "I don't know," I replied, stupidly. "Well, he thought that you stole it, and when I told him that you didn't, he said that I was a liar. Then he called me Jew. Our last name's Finestein, you see. He said that you stole it and I sold it, because I was a Jew. Dennis' friend, Tom, found the board on the beach, and brought it to us while we were arguing. He became even madder when he saw the ding in his board." I didn't say anything.

Thinking that we would be gone before Dennis found me, I continued picking weeds with my knife. She opened the greasy sack, reached in, pulled out a chicken wing and began eating. I reached over to take a piece of chicken for myself, but she stopped my hand, saying, "You can have it, if you say that you're sorry for hitting me yesterday." When I said that I was sorry, she held the sack out to me and I reached in, and pulled out the tiniest drumstick I had ever seen. The meat was good and I told her that I was sorry again. She offered me the sack again, smiling and almost laughing as I bit into the meat. Then she let go with a laugh and asked me, "How do you like your rabbit, Jack? "Jackrabbit," I said, laughing a little. When she didn't laugh, I said, "Jackrabbit, get it, jackrabbit!" She smiled and nodded and laughed again. I asked her if it was my rabbit, she said it was, and I thought that it was pretty good, and didn't complain about it.

I went into Grandma's kitchen and made cherry Kool-Aid from a package that I had bought the day before, mixing it in the big tin pitcher with a wooden spoon, adding extra sugar and big chunks of ice. Back on the lawn, we continued pouring drinks, until we had finished the entire pitcher of Kool-Aid and there was nothing left of the rabbit but bones. We lay there, holding hands, looking up at the sky, and laughing. We stood up and she took her jackknife from her pocket, ready to play a game of stretch with me. Before she even made the first throw, I heard my name being called from the street. It was the Dennis, and he was riding his bike, with Tom. "Hey, Jew Girl, get away from your boyfriend, I'm going to pound him," shouted Dennis. I said nothing as they pulled up close enough for us to hear their hard breathing. They sat on their bikes, looking at me. I told him that I was sorry about the board, and reached into my pocket for the remaining four dollars and change that I had leeched on the pier, offering it as payment for the ding. He took the money, but he didn't care about the board anymore. He was here to fight.

They laid their bikes against the curb and stood their ground, saying nasty things to me, and calling Sarah "Jew" and "kike." I wanted to run away into the house, but Sarah stood her ground. Trying to be bold, I stood as tall as I could, next to her. Dennis picked up a rock from the street, and threw it at Sarah. Moving slightly to one side, the rock barely missed her face. I was shaking, but she was calm, touching the gold star around her neck.

"Jack, I'm gonna' kick your ass," shouted Dennis. Tom repeated Dennis' words, rolled up his sleeves and pulled a stick from his bike rack. "Don't move, keep looking at them, and show no fear," Sarah whispered to me. Slowly, she reached down and picked up a big rock from the edge of the flowerbed, clenching the rock so tightly that her fingers turned white. She was deadly with rocks and could hit whatever she aimed at. Fear came on me fast and I turned and ran toward the house with no thought of helping her. She stood alone on the grass, facing them, holding onto the rock. They came up from the gutter, onto the curb and up the sidewalk.

Before I reached the steps to the house, I saw the back of Grandmother's head. She was deaf, watching TV, and her gray hair reminded me of my grandfather, Jose.

"Be bold," I could almost hear his words, almost feel him next to me. "Be bold," I said aloud. "Bold as a lion," I shouted. Then boldness ran through me and I turned and ran into the garage to get the bow and arrows. When I returned, I stood just behind Sarah. Dennis and Tom were right in front of her now. They inched slowly forward, yelling thief at me, and Jew at Sarah, who was innocent of everything. Dennis leaned forward and shoved her, and she moved back, but didn't fall and remained silent. They were still yelling and Sarah was standing straight, holding tightly onto the rock, waiting for them to move before she threw it. As they started forward again, I took an arrow from the sheaf, pulled it tightly against the bowstring, and pointed it directly at Dennis' heart. Then they quit coming at us.

When I walked up next to her, she pulled her shoulders back and continued to stare them down. "Get out of here, Dennis, or I'll kill you," I yelled, feeling all of the power of Jose in my words. Dennis and Tom were silent now. They didn't move forward, but they didn't move backwards either. Sarah never budged. "I swear to God, I'll kill you just like I killed that rabbit," I shouted, motioning with my head to the clean wet bones lying on the lawn, near his bare feet.

Dennis didn't like being backed down, especially when it was a girl and when that girl was a Jew. Still, he wouldn't take a chance this time; he could feel the rage of Jose and he knew that I would run him through if he got any closer. I pulled the string as tight as it would go, hoping and praying that it would not break. If my fingers slipped, Dennis was dead. If the string broke, we were finished. He back peddled slowly, making his way off the lawn, to the curb, then to the gutter, where his bike lay. Tom was right beside him. I kept the arrow on Dennis, and Sarah kept the rock tight in her hand. Together, they lifted their bikes from the gutter, got up and rode away. As soon as they began peddling, I lifted the arrow and shot it straight up, into the air, not knowing where it would land. Luck was strong then and the arrow flew high before rocketing back down, barely missing Dennis. I fired another arrow and it fell just beyond Tom. They peddled faster. When Dennis turned around and saw that I had lowered the bow, he yelled "Jew" one final time to Sarah. Then she let fly the rock, and it whistled through the air and skipped over the hot tar road, until it hit its mark, low on the boy's back tire, which caused the wheel to wobble. He hit the street like a sack of potatoes.

I laughed as she picked up another rock from the flowerbed, and walked slowly toward the cowering boy. She stood above him, his body shaking, lying on the street as she held the rock in her cocked fist, staring down at the boy who called for his friend, Tom. But Tom was long gone. Clumsily, Dennis got up on his bike, and rode away. Sarah dropped the rock in the street, and once out of range, Dennis turned around and yelled out "You'll be sorry, Jack." I lifted my bow and tried to send another arrow in his direction, but the string snapped and the arrow remained, harmlessly, in my hand.

"My name's Jessie," I shouted, hoping that Dennis could hear me, and never forget that he had been defeated by a Mexican boy and a Jewish girl. He grew small in the distance and didn't turn around again. Sarah and I laughed hard now, and I reached over and kissed her on the cheek. Then, I kissed her on the lips again and again, and she put her long, beautiful arms around me and pulled me down, onto the grass, kissing and laughing for hours until it was nearly dark, and we gathered our things and said goodbye to Grandmother.

It was a lucky day and we got a quick ride in a pickup truck in just a few minutes. She had some cookies in her backpack that we shared as we sat in the bed of the truck, happy, afraid of nothing in the world, then falling asleep in each other's arms for about an hour as the warm summer wind blew through our dreams. It was a good ride, and the man took us almost all the way home.

Sarah *is a chapter in an upcoming novel by Chris Ahrens, titled,* The Miracle Of The Train.

BETWEEN HEAVEN AND EARTH

It was a warm El Niño morning as I followed Skip Frye up the 17 step metal ladder, to what he called "the crow's nest," a platform that stood, until recently, above Harry's Surf Shop, and the surf line. From this vantage point, the West Coast's most dedicated surfer could be seen, checking the surf every morning, for ten years. Directly beneath us is one of Southern California's last bastions of soul, where the whine of Frye's planer, or that of his partner, Hank Warner, were heard on a daily basis. Out front, Donna Frye sells surfboards and a few related items, while going about her business of Surfers Tired Of Pollution (STOP), whose primary purpose is that of preserving ocean quality.

On this day the swell is huge, perhaps the biggest of the decade, focusing on a reef a mile or so beyond the regular lineup at Pacific Beach Point, a spot that Frye has ruled for over 40 years. "That's Little Makaha," he says, motioning with his head, wondering at the size of the massive hump that continues peeling, leaving a thick carpet of whitewater behind it. The next wave swings wide, and duplicates the previous one. Four or five more waves sheet off in succession, like an oversized Malibu. "I don't know what that's called," says Frye. "I've never seen it break before. It might be the spot that Don Okey talks about, where he and Woody Brown used to surf." The comment takes me out of the moment and back to the early '40s, when Okey, Brown, Dempsey, Skeeter, Barber, Cromwell, Lloyd Baker, Woody Ekstrom, Dorian Paskowitz, Storm Surf Taylor and very few others were out exploring the then remote shoreline of San Diego for the biggest surf that they could find.

The wave fires again, and I imagine the boys sliding tall for half a mile on their planks. If not here, they might have been down at Tijuana Sloughs, North Bird or La Jolla Cove. Maybe Windansea if it was holding.

Unfortunately '40s surfing went by largely undocumented, as there were few cameras around, and nobody had the lens power to see very far out into the Pacific. Another wave hits the deep-water reef, bends toward shore and peels into the channel. It's becoming too much for Frye, and he wonders aloud about where to lineup, should he decide to paddle out. It would be an effort, even on a modern surfboard, something that helps me to realize what great watermen our forebears were. Frye passes me the binoculars and I watch yet another wave, Xeroxed right down to the spit, without an uneven section. He hints at paddling out, and I know that I'll have to join him if he does. It's not a decision that he takes lightly, even though he is equipped with four tenths of a century of wave-riding knowledge, a surf fax saying that the swell has peaked and surf craft that not even Woody Brown had dreamed of half a century earlier. I have that sick feeling you get just before entering something you're unsure of. A broken leash would send me on the longest ocean swim of my life. Frye goes silent and takes a few deep breaths. He seems ready, and I am reminded of that poster of him knee-paddling out at Cojo. I'll have a similar view if I follow him out.

Frye's personal rhythm is a lot like the ocean's, a smooth, steady flow without hard lines. No jump starts. All liquid lubricated parts. I have seen him surf since the mid-1960s, when he helped to define California soul, and became synonymous with the term, soul surfing. By the late '60s he was heavily into Vee bottoms, corresponding regularly with Australian surf pioneer, Bob McTavish about the new machines. The "Fryed" egg era took up a great deal of the '70s, and, once again, the board fit his style perfectly. This blended into the Lis Fish era. I don't recall ever seeing Frye on standard trifins, but he was among the first to build boards for the longboard renaissance of the '70s. Some say that he should be the only person allowed to ride his 12 footers, where he practices cross-country surfing, riding up to a dozen breaks in a single session.

Big waves slow everything down. You can spot a set wave, start a conversation, and not be finished by the time it breaks. There never seems to be a hurry when the waves are bigger than is comfortable, and we stand there talking about what boards would work, where to paddle out, how long the paddle might take and what to expect when getting caught inside. Frye's big boards seem ideal, since the waves we're contemplating can shift 100 yards at a time. Suddenly, the outside sets quit. Apparently this is a tide sensitive spot. Half an hour later, the waves simply peak and roll past the reef. I like to think that I would have gone out, but maybe not. Maybe I would have sat in the channel, watching Frye glide like a bird, disappearing from sight. And maybe I would have ridden some of the best waves of my life. I'll never know.

Frye decides to go back to work and I drive north, toward home, wondering all the while if I could have ridden those waves, and how the next time I see them break I might be too old to even think about paddling out.

DODO

Dodo, that's how the man introduced himself to us that morning when he showed up at our door in Paia, Maui, without shoes or shirt, in flowered shorts, holding a pillowcase stuffed full of dirty laundry. He had grown up on Maui, and was half Hawaiian, half good natured, and while he looked at least 30, he had the mind of a child, crying when he told us that his parents didn't want him any more and that he had no place to go. He fit right in with the rest of us.

Danny had been the first to notice the old house, hidden amid years of weeds, just outside of the little town. He took a cycle to the overgrowth, cleared the trash, tore out and replaced some of the bad wood, plastered the walls, plastic wrapped the broken windows, drove out most of the rats and evil spirits, and moved in without paying rent or telling the owners, a corporate group from Texas who saw the island paradise as one hell of an investment. When I stumbled upon Danny's house in July of 1969, there were over 30 surfers, all of them Danny's guests, scattered throughout the 12 bedrooms. I took my spot on the living room floor, occasionally breaking through the rotten wood on my way to the moldy bathroom. Even then, you could see by her fine curves that she had once been a beautiful estate, accented by stained glass and linen, probably the crown jewel of some large sugarcane plantation. Like everything in that volcanic soil, it was quick to rise and quick to return to the earth, crumbling, one balcony, one Victorian parlor at a time. Dodo found peace and comfort sleeping on the couch, on the front porch.

Dodo was afraid of the ocean, and he didn't surf. He did, however, admire surfers, and he would wax our boards, and help us to carry them to Hookipa Park. He followed us everywhere, always trying to please us by helping out. There were usually problems with his helping, however, like the time he attempted to make all 30 of us pancakes, using a full bag of sugar instead of flour, smoking out the kitchen, catching some of the cabinets on fire and nearly burning the place down before we put out the flames with damp beach towels. When Danny found Dodo, he was 40 feet up, huddled in the tree house, crying and scared that he was in trouble. When he finally came down, he submitted to Danny's gentle reprimand, and a few of us walked him into town to treat him to a 45-cent bowel of Top Ramen at Larry's. Dodo was our friend.

I don't remember seeing them approach, but one day there were tractors parked in the yard, steel teeth gleaming, ready to feast on Danny's house, and it occurred to most everyone that they would need to move out and pay rent someplace. This also meant finding work, which was a problem for people who hated work, especially when there was none. Tourism had yet to boom on the island, and there were lines waiting to inherit even dishwashing positions. We were getting hungry and worried when Dodo walked into the house with a flier from a big movie company, saying that they needed extras for a picture called *The Hawaiians*, a sequel, as it turned out, to the movie *Hawaii*, starring Charlton Heston and Geraldine Chaplin. A small cheap facade of Hawaiian city (similar in construction to the condos that would soon overwhelm Maui) had been built at our favorite summer surf spot, Maalaea, an impossible wall that the magazine would later call "The Fastest Wave In The World."

I had surfed Maalaea with nobody but Herbie Fletcher out earlier in the year, and watched him get further down the line than I thought possible. Now, it was flat, and the land was dotted with movie cameras, movie people and catering trucks. The old clipper ship, Carthaginian, was docked in the harbor, after having made the trip around the point, from Lahaina, where it had been a dormant tourist attraction for decades.

My friend Ralph, Dodo and I signed the necessary papers, and were sent to get our costumes, the tattered rags of the town's folks for Ralph and I, and, because he was Hawaiian, the costume of a leper for Dodo, who took great pride in going to makeup and getting scars on his face. Lepers were lucky. They got more money, worked more days and had a chance to sail on the ship.

Each day at work, Ralph would tease the simple-minded Dodo about his makeup, asking him if he had fallen and hurt himself. Then Dodo would point angrily to the makeup man saying, "He did it, stupid." Dodo had a still photo taken with Charlton Heston, who was very nice to everyone, and would stand still for any photo, no matter who wanted it.

One afternoon, it became apparent to Ralph and I that the swell was increasing, watching tiny 100 mph waves peel perfectly from the jetty, to infinity. We were among hundreds of extras, and, hoping that nobody would spot us, we tore out of our costumes, down to our trunks, which we always wore as underpants, and paddled out, driving down the line for 50 or 60 yards before being swatted by the zippering lip. We returned in time to change into our costumes, and do a scene that involved loading Dodo and the other lepers onto the ship.

In the scene, Heston pushed Dodo aside, and Dodo reacted by turning around and screaming for him to "knock off the rough stuff." Dodo soon realized that it was Moses, the star of *The Ten Commandments*, who had pushed him, and he became apologetic, offering to cook "Mister Heston," as he called him, pancakes. Heston wisely declined. On the next take, Dodo anticipated the push, and fell to the ground before Heston even touched him. Now, approaching take three, the director was getting a little nervous. "Okay, we're going to do this again, are there any questions?" Dodo raised his hand and said, "You better hurry up, because the sun's going down." It was no joke to Dodo, but everybody, including Heston and the director laughed, before the star slapped Dodo affectionately on the shoulder. The scene went perfectly, the sun went down, and we all went home, Ralph and I listening to Dodo retell his unintentional joke again and again, as I drove. "You better hurry up, because the sun's going down."

The next day Ralph and I were told that we were no longer needed on the set, and I sneaked into makeup to get a few scars, with the hope of falling in with the lepers and riding on the boat. I nearly made it, but was turned back by some assistant director just before the cameras began rolling, when he removed my hat and discovered that I was a *haole*. That was the end of my movie career, but I continued to drive Dodo out to the set each day, for two more weeks, where he worked on land and aboard ship, and eventually was on board for the sailing back to Lahaina.

I picked up Dodo at the dock one evening, noticing a lot of nervous people, but no ship. Dodo was angry, saying that some dumbbell had sunk the boat, and put him out of work. He would be recalled in a week or so, when the boat was resurrected. He sulked all the way home, where I got my board and walked to Hookipa Park, and he accompanied me to the beach, his star status affecting him to the point that he no longer offered to wax my board.

The destruction crew had moved in that day and taken out all of the old trees, and everybody moved out of the old house except Dodo, Ralph and I. The next morning we had breakfast on the porch, watching the big trees and the tree house topple, until all of the land around Danny's house had been scraped flat. The vegetable garden and a rickety gazebo were the last things standing between the bulldozers and our home. While we had ignored every eviction notice, the Maui sheriffs had now come to get us out at gunpoint, if necessary.

We packed our few belongings into my Falcon wagon, our new home, and drove away without looking back, none of us wanting to see the old house get beaten by the angry machines. As we drove up the coast to Hookipa, Dodo napped in the car. That night we cooked hotdogs under the pavilion, and bedded down early. Ralph and Dodo shared the folded down back seat of the wagon, while I curled up in the front seat, with two mosquito coils burning near my head, getting devoured by the insects anyway, before falling into a deep sleep, and waking abruptly to a harsh light. It was one of the local cops.

"What are you guys doing here?" he asked.

"We're on vacation," snapped Ralph, sarcastically.

"Are you on vacation, or just bumming around, I know the difference," said the sheriff.

"Okay, what's the difference?" said Ralph.

The cop decided that we really were bumming around, and said that he'd be back in half an hour to run us in if we weren't gone. Dodo, who had been asleep the entire time, pulled his head from the hole of his sleeping bag and looked into the harsh light, frowning. Then, "Hey, uncle, howzit?"

"Dodo, what are you doing here?" asked the cop.

"I live here, uncle. These are my friends."

The cop was nearly apologetic now, thanking us for taking care of his nephew, and giving Dodo a fat wad of one-dollar bills, with the admonition that he take care of himself. He said goodbye, got back into the car and drove away. We slept soundly, and were up early to ride the tiny surf. Then Ralph forced Dodo out into the water on his surfboard, and pushed him into a small whitewater wave. Dodo was unable to get to his feet, but he did feel the joy of moving on a wave, and he was happy for the rest of the day.

Within a week, Ralph had gone back to the Mainland, leaving me alone to attend to Dodo. Soon, Dodo got tired of living in the car and eating nothing but wild fruit, fish, and vegetables. His back was sore and he was covered in mosquito bites. He wanted a home, a real home, he said. I was already losing my patience, and now Dodo was beginning to act strangely, even for him. He said that he wanted to go to the old house. When he continued to insist that we go back there, I drove him onto the dirt of the now vacant lot to prove that the place was gone. He said that I had gone to the wrong place. "Where's the tree house, and the garden, and the big house, and where is my friend, Danny? I want to see Danny." He cried tears that I couldn't cry for the old house, and then he began shouting about the old house and Danny and Top Ramen at Larry's. No matter how I tried, I couldn't convince him that the house was no longer there. He tried to hit me, and screamed in my face that I was a liar. Then, he ran out of the car. I was so angry with him that I let him go. When I finally calmed down and went looking for him again, he had disappeared into the blackness of the night.

The next day I moved into Animal Farm in Lahaina, where I lived for a month or so. One evening after dinner at the Lahaina Bakery, I spotted Dodo walking the street in a pressed white shirt, navy blue slacks and black, polished leather shoes.

He was with two over dressed, stern-faced men. I approached him and said hello, but he had a distant look and was unable to recognize me. He had obviously been medicated, and the men were his guardians. I asked them about Dodo, and they told me his real name. I recognized the unusual last name as that of a hotel builder who lived on Maui. They said that he had recently run away from the sanitarium, and they laughed, saying that he had some crazy ideas about being a movie star and a surfer.

That winter, Honolua Bay exploded with the swell of the century and I broke two boards in three days. I limped back to California that spring, located Ralph, and we drank wine at my parent's home, before going to Hollywood to see the newly released movie, *The Hawaiians* at The Egyptian Theater, staring Charlton Heston. The story was set in old Hawaii, and we listened as Heston delivered his lines about the future of the Hawaiian people, that seemed ironic to us, since we had seen their end and knew that they were as doomed as the American Indians. I thought that I saw myself in one of the crowd scenes, and Ralph tried to point out his half second of fame. Then we watched with pride to clearly see Dodo being shoved by Heston, and falling to the ground convincingly. Ralph and I gave Dodo a standing ovation, right in the middle of the movie. A man seated behind us told us to sit down and keep quiet. We complied, realizing that he didn't understand what a great performance he had just seen.

KING OF THE SURF GUITAR

It wasn't my fault that my father had left the beach and moved inland the year that I was born. I had nothing to do with it, but I learned early on that it's best to fess up to such things before other people discover them. So, here goes: In 1963 I was an inlander. I was also a hodad, a kook and a gremmie. With high ambitions of becoming a good surfer, I joined the Monterey Park Surf Club, which was made up entirely of inlanders and mostly of kooks. My brother, Dave, and I were pledging the club, sitting around the park with about a dozen of its members, lying about our surfing experiences, when the club secretary, Chickie, looked at the clipboard in his lap and began asking questions:
"How long have you been surfing?"
"What is your favorite surf spot?"
"Are you a good noserider?"
"Do you like big waves?"

We lied our way through the interview without comment from the others. Then we were asked, "Who's the best surfer in the world?" Nearly half of the club members whispered the name Phil Edwards. One guy said Dewey Weber. Someone else said Donald Takayama. Butch Van Artsdalen got honorable mention. Chickie ordered everyone to be quiet, looked at Dave and I and asked again: "Who's the best surfer in the world?" We huddled together for a moment and then came out and said, in a united voice, "Dick Dale."

"Dick Dale!" said Chickie, with a laugh. "He's a hodad." The others were divided, some saying that Dale was the best or among the best, while others said that he really was a hodad. Nobody there argued, however, that he was the hottest guitar player in the world. As I recall, neither Dave nor I made the cut, and somehow managed to have a good time surfing without all of those people to go along with us. We never lost our faith in Dick Dale, however.

It was our older sister, Jackie, who brought home

Surfer's Choice, the first LP by the man who would become known as the king of the surf guitar. The music pumped stoke like a big north swell, and I spent hours carpet surfing to *Surf Beat, Miserlou* and *Mile Zero*, while setting the record cover on top of the hi-fi, imitating the photo taken of the king as he slid a Dana Point wall.

Every Saturday night, Jackie and her friends went to a surfer stomp, either at Retail Clerk's, The Rendezvous, or Harmony Park. I was only in ninth grade, and had never been to a dance of any sort, when she asked me if I wanted to go to Harmony Park with her, where her favorite band, Dick Dale and The Deltones was playing. I was too stoked for words. The first thing I did was to wrinkle my Madras plaid shit and white Levis. Then, I ran my new Converse through the mud, washed the grease from my hair and combed it to the side. The band tore it up that night as surfers, posers, hodads and gremmies united without knowing who could surf and who could not. It was a big moment for me.

Twenty years later: A young surfer named Chris O'Rourke is living and dying with Hodkin's Disease at a home in Encinitas, when the idea of a musical fund-raiser comes up, to help pay the surfer's mounting medical bills. Some talented local musicians offer their services. The La Paloma Theater donates their facility. San Diego radio stations lend their support with free air play, and surfers from Imperial Beach to Oceanside scrape together five bucks for a ticket.

I wish that I could remember who had his phone number. Anyway, somebody connected me to the private line of Dick Dale, one of the biggest influences in my kook's life. Before I dialed, I flashed on the gremmie years, lying awake three nights in a row, after seeing him at Harmony Park and later on the Rendezvous Ballroom, the moves of the Surfer Stomp still fresh in my mind.

He answered the phone himself, and listened patiently as I, a complete stranger, stumbled through the introductions, and revealed that California's best surfer was fighting for his life. He heard me out, before informing me that his wife was scheduled for surgery on the day of the concert, and that he had to be with her. He hoped that I would understand; he just couldn't make it. I thanked him for his time.

Less than an hour later, Dale called back to say that his wife had rescheduled her surgery, in order to accommodate the benefit, and that he, she and the entire band would play the La Paloma. I can still recall the force of his words as he added, "Any surfer who won't spend five dollars for this kid, isn't worth the wax he stands on." The man showed up, and he and his band rocked the joint hard. I introduced myself to him backstage, and he said that he hoped that he had helped the cause. The band broke down their equipment, and he disappeared like the super hero that he is. Our grateful town was left vibrating in his wake, and I realized once and for all that Dick Dale was the king of the surf guitar, and, definitely no hodad.

AFTER THE FALL

Mister Trent had been the 12th grade science teacher at Newman's Academy for nearly 35 years. In that time he had seen duck tails flop and flattops fray, to the point where boys and girls became nearly indistinguishable from each other, to him. By the time he became used to long hair, along came unisexual buzz cuts. This trend was followed by long, short, buzzed, combed, colored, parted and spiked, all at once. Through Eisenhower, Kennedy, Johnson, Nixon, Ford, Carter, Reagan, Bush, Clinton, then Bush and Clinton again, one thing remained constant —Mister Trent's standard military crewcut, which went in and out of style countless times while he was at Newman's.

He was an inventor, a genius who could build anything with paperclips and chewing gum, but had never once switched on a computer, believing that the human brain, his in particular, was superior to any machine. His vast knowledge of science and surfing amused three and a half generations of students. They laughed whenever he rolled up to school in his 1952 Chevy pickup, with his newest surf-related invention snug in its bed, before they paddled out on their cookie cutter six-two thrusters and practiced the same cutback for five years. The more creative among them were only adventurous enough to attempt some pin wing design, fashioned twenty-five years earlier. Among Mister Trent's quiver were boards with solar-powered motors, retractable fins, no fins, spring loaded fins and fish scales. Some of the surfboards had holes running through them, one had a gel pack sandwiched between the foam. There were boards with two and three hulls, and other strange designs. While each board was different in shape, they were all similar in construction. Built from California yucca and discarded plastic, the teacher's *Apocalypse Surfboards* bore no resemblance to the resin lollipops found in surf shops worldwide. Of course his unorthodox style earned the old man nicknames. "Bent Trent," "The Mad Scientist," and, because of his straight ahead, practical surfing style, "Straight Ahead Ted," were among them.

Like most people who mind their own business and enjoy life to the fullest, Mister Trent never realized that he was a weirdo. He played and worked hard each day, gently transferring scientific knowledge into rigid craniums. He was so good at his job that few of his students even realized that they were being taught anything. His classrooms always echoed with riotous shouts, laugher and explosions that sometimes rocked the entire campus. Still, Mister Trent's students scored well above the national average each year in science, and each of them developed a working application of the subject that they carried into adult life.

While he was an open book of scientific knowledge, his personal life was closed. Nobody ever knew that his wife of 30 years had recently died, and left him to live alone in the hills, where he enjoyed a completely self-contained life—growing his own food, watering crops from his own wells, raising eggs and chickens, and getting all of his electricity from his own home-built solar panels and windmills. The students never knew this, and they never cared. To them Mister Trent was a cartoon character who ceased to exist the moment that he walked out the door at three o'clock each day.

The world's computer systems didn't crash on January 1, 2000 as some people had predicted they would. No. They played a far nastier trick on the world, frying when nobody expected them to, exactly five years later, at the turn of midnight, on January 1, 2005. It was worse than anybody thought it could be —water didn't run, gas didn't pump, electricity didn't surge through the lines. Some said it would be six months before anything could be done about it. Mister Trent knew that it would take much longer. Some starved and some froze to death, but most deaths were related to looting and fear. Within minutes the world had been sent back to the 19th century. Life had instantly changed for every American, except the Amish and Mister Trent, who stayed home and lived as he always had, fishing from his surfboard through sunrises and sunsets, growing things and inventing things. He sunk a new well and converted his truck to run on the alcohol that he distilled from the potatoes he grew.

He enjoyed the new world. There was no traffic, and surfers, who had become dependent upon the Internet for wave predictions, missed entire swells. Without a job to go to, Mister Trent's surf sessions lasted for five or six hours each day. Those first two weeks in January were among the best of his life. One day he realized that he had left his welder at the school. His two hour commute had been cut to a pleasant 25 minutes.

Mister Trent was a careful, calculating man, rarely surprised by anything. Upon entering the school that day, however, he saw something that truly amazed him—seven members of the student body—four girls: Tammy, Courtney, Ashley and Brittany and three boys: David, Jay, and Steven, were huddled close together, trying to stay warm. The cans of food that had been collected for but not delivered to the homeless were scattered across the floor, after their contents had been devoured, cold. Glass splinters were scattered over the tile floor after the soda machine had been broken into for its contents.

It was the first time in years that anyone had used the schoolteacher's proper name, and now it came from an unlikely source. "Mister Trent," shouted Steve, a rail thin long hair known as "Rocker" because of his vast CD collection and air guitar shows. Everyone in the classroom turned slowly, Jay raising Ashley's head, and offering the hopeful words, "Mister Trent's here." The girl smiled before lying back down to rest again. The teacher held the back of his hand against the girl's forehead, jumped up, opened a cabinet door, and blended a concoction of several elements, which he forced the girl to drink. To the amazement of everyone excluding the teacher, but including the grateful girl, she was up and around within half an hour.

The man now went back to his truck and quickly returned with bags of fruit and nuts, which the students choked down. If any of them had looked closely, they would have seen a tear in his eye. After they had eaten and their minds had cleared, the teacher asked his students why they were not at home. The usually model thin, now concentration camp thin "Ashley the Anorexic," as she was called, answered for them all. "When the power went out, our parents didn't know what to do. We always went out to eat, and there was very little food stored at home. They didn't know how to get anything from the land, so rather than starve, we came looking for you, hoping that you would be here and show us how to survive. Our parents came to get us, but they didn't know what to do. John and Judy went with them, but the rest of decided to stay here, with each other."

"Forget about your parents, we've got work to do," snapped Mister Trent. "Steven, help me put my welder into the truck. You others, gather any food, wood, blankets and pads that you can find, and meet us outside." Rocker's arms shook as he attempted lifting the welding tanks, and Jay was called upon to replace him. Disguising hurt feelings, Rocker shrugged his shoulders, went to the truck and made himself a comfortable place in the bed, while the others gathered supplies. The ride out was so happy that they sang Christmas carols, even though it was two months past the season.

With seven more bodies to feed, there was lots of work to be done—extra planting, fishing, farming and building. Everyone did their share, except for Rocker, who tried to be funny in order to compensate for his laziness and win the affection of Ashley, who had no use at all for an air guitarist in this situation. Ashley was beginning to put on weight, and feel good. She hadn't felt so good since she was a girl, and she used to catch butterflies in the fields behind her home. That was before her father made a killing in the stock market. He was a reporter for the local paper then, not well off, and she wore second hand clothes to school. She could still fell the pain of seventh grade, other girls singing "Ashley, Ashley pencil thin, gets her clothes from the garbage bin." She had not been liberated from the fashion cycle until coming here, where it didn't matter what you wore, or how much money you had, only what you did to keep yourself and the others alive. Already, the young girl had learned many useful skills, including how to trap lobster, how to fish and how to operate the still, which made fuel for the truck. Rocker, of course, had other purposes for the still, and was given extra duty by Mister Trent when he was caught making a little home brew.

After the first month, false nails, jewelry, cosmetics and high-heeled shoes had been voluntarily abandoned in the scrap heap, where Mister Trent would reincarnate them into useful items. Within two months there was no fat on any of the students, and the skinny among them had put on enough muscle to dig postholes and swing axes. After three months, everybody but Rocker (who's nickname had been changed to Talker) was enjoying the new life, getting up early to surf in the cold water, before coming home to pump water, cut and mill wood and raise food. As time went by, all of the children became tough and independent, never thinking about the plugged in life of home, each in turn expressing hopes that the computers would never be fixed, and that they could live like this forever.

Rocker, who had been the most popular boy in the school, was treated like a nerd on the ranch. Mister Trent, who had been treated like a nerd in school, was a god, or at least a major rock star on the ranch. When the batteries died for Rocker's disk player, he was like someone waking from a deep sleep. He noticed the sounds of birds, and wind and rain, and listened to the conversations of others. Mister Trent taught him the basics of the guitar, and within time, Rocker learned a few cords. Then he began to sing, and to write a few songs. He had been diagnosed as hyperactive, and had been medicated since he was in the fourth grade. Without medication, he turned his energy into work, and was soon up early, surfing, and digging and planting, working the fat from his soul.

Over time, each of the girls fell in love with Mister Trent. He was decent man, however, and kept a proper distance, sleeping alone, beneath the awning of the ranch house. This isolation had caused the children to become less well supervised than he had intended. When one of the girls became pregnant, Mister Trent delivered a boy, and the girl named him Trent.

As they became more efficient, the days were filled with short hours of work and long hours of play, which included fishing, little made-up games and surfing. The nights were spent around the fire, studying the stars through Mister Trent's telescope, or looking toward the vanished lights of the city, a sure signal that the computer problem had yet to be fixed. The years of darkness directly corresponded to the illumination of the students, and none of them wanted to leave, except for Ashley, who confided to Ted, which was how everyone now addressed Mister Trent, that she wanted to see her mother again.

The man drove the girl down the hill, to the once posh neighborhood, that now resembled a movie about the fall of Rome. The fake pillars were all cracked or broken and entire structures had been burned to the ground, after the homes had been looted. Because they had some real life skills, the Mexican servants and gardeners fled to the hills to work the land, where some of their former masters were invited to live, and learn to work with their hands. Many a yuppie took their own lives, sat idly, or cut into the food lines set up by the Red Cross, because they still believed in their own superiority. Ashley found her mother barely clinging to life amid the torn imported silk drapes and concrete statues of angels. A band of marauding skateboarders could be heard, sweeping through the suburb like a pack of wild dogs. Even now, they broke into houses, seeking whatever food might be stored here and there. Ashley's mother had long been divorced from her 70 hour a week father. The woman, Anne, who had once been a runner-up in the Miss America pageant, was not spared because of her undiminished good looks, but because of the family gun that she kept near the door. She had scared off the looters before, but now she was running low on bullets, and she feared for her life. She was one of the last adults on her block to stay in the neighborhood, living on eucalyptus tea, the fruits of the orange trees that had been planted by her and her neighbors as a tax write off, and the strawberries planted everywhere, for ornamental purposes. The last meat she had eaten came from the duck she found and shot in the swimming pool, the fish from the aquarium, and the roasting of Tuffy, the family's standard poodle.

Mister Trent took the woman back to his home, and there nursed her to health on wild berries, nuts and seafood. Within a week she was feeling strong again, trading her designer aerobic shores for a pair of sturdy and warm boots that Mister Trent had made from a raccoon that a coyote had killed. In time the woman leaned how to cut firewood, plant seed and tend a garden. She became the best fisher in the group, bringing back strings of corbina from the shore. She became a decent surfer, and stayed in the water, laughing and playing for hours with Mister Trent and his students.

The power came back on more than three years after it went off, and people slowly began to migrate back to the cities and put their trust in wonders that they were not connected to. It took another two years before the malls began to fill up with people desperate for Japanese animation cards, floral dust ruffles, caviar spoons, and matching kitty shower curtains and soap dishes. All of the children, except for Ashley and Rocker, eventually returned to finish school. The couple, that is what they had become, stayed on the ranch with Mister and Misses Trent, the name that Ashley's mother used after being wed on a clear Saturday morning near the creek. A week later, Ashley and Steven were married in a beautiful ceremony, witnessed by God, a dozen chickens, two horses and a barn owl. Someday you may make a wrong turn and stumble across an elderly couple and a younger couple with three beautiful children all living without status, address, telephone, television, electrical power, house payments or stress in a quiet corner of California. If you do, show them respect; they've been through a lot.

SCOOTER BOY

Scooter Boy is known as one of the greatest hot-dog surfers ever from Waikiki. And while his small wave surfing is legendary, his skill in big surf has largely gone unreported, until now. A fantastic surfer himself, John Peck remembers meeting Scooter at Waikiki in the late 1950s. He was a little older, but still an amazing surfer in a place filled with amazing surfers. Asked about riding big surf, Scooter told Peck about a day at Kaena Point when he paddled out from Yokohama and rode waves that were four olo boards high (the average olo board was about 16 feet high.) Do the math.

SCHOOLING

Jay had been given two great gifts from his father on his tenth birthday. One was a pool table. The other was a series of lessons in the game from the man who had made a living with a stick throughout his 20's. Jay's dad showed his boy how to bank balls and line up shots. Later he would learn tricks, like suckering an opponent into sinking the eight ball, and fancy jump shots. As it had to his father, pool became more than just a game to Jay. It became an obsession that would, like it had for his father, provide an income for him in the young portion of his life. He had a four-digit savings account when the rest of us were trying to squeeze an extra quarter allowance out of our parents. At 17, he had won every small tournament in town, and on Friday nights, while the rest of us were at parties, he went to the bowling alley, playing pool with anyone who dared challenge him. Once when the great Willy Masconi came to town, Jay played him and lost, but not by much.

Big Jim, the owner of the town's new Chrysler dealership, considered himself quite a sportsman. He had the heads of the animals he had shot in Africa, stuffed and mounted in the showroom. He never tired of telling how he won the big game for the local high school team, the Cardinals, with his winning touchdown pass against the Pirates. He handled a pool stick pretty well too, but the drunker he became, the worse he got and the better he considered himself to be. He was a loud mouth, and nobody liked him, and now he was quite drunk and still fairly on his game, taking big bills from everybody foolish enough to play against him. "I'll bet a hundred bucks I can beat anyone here," he hollered, slapping a hundred on the table and staring in Jay's direction. Nick and Vic, the two Russian brothers who watched over things at the pool hall, each threw down fifty on Big Jim's table. Nick, who was the better player of the two brothers, quickly lost the money, and Jim grew louder as he became more confident. Jay just kept playing alone in the corner, making impossible shots that Big Jim ignored as he drank and leaned on his cue before floating over to Jay's corner while the boy went quietly about the business of clearing the table.

Jay never looked up as Big Jim shouted, "Come on, kid, I could use another hundred." Jim slapped a wrinkled bill onto the felt. "Gambling's illegal, sir," Jay said politely, motioning with his head to the "No Gambling" sign, before returning to his game. Then I saw Jay miss an easy shot. Big Jim saw it too, and I knew what was up. The big man made some lewd remarks and put another hundred down, saying, "Okay, two hundred!" Jay continued playing, barely missing combination shots that nobody but him could make. Pausing, looking up, Jay said, "Besides, I don't have two hundred dollars." Nick the Russian quickly pulled a hundred and two fifties from the fat leather wallet he kept in his vest pocket and laid them on the table, beside Big Jim's money. The Russian racked the balls.

The man broke with a powerful stroke, sinking two stripes. He followed that with two more stripes, and missed a difficult shot. He left Jay with nothing but a satisfied grin as he sat down. He wouldn't get up again until Jay had cleared the table of all but two solids and the eight ball. Big Jim sunk one more ball, and left the kid to win the game. Nick and Jay each pocketed a hundred and, thinking this was the end of it, Jay went back to dropping balls quietly at his own table. Big Jim was furious. "Double or nothing, you son of a bitch," he shouted. Jay looked to Nick who nodded, and laid the bet on the rail. This time Jay put on a display that would have sent any rational man, drunk or sober, into horseshoes.

Nick and Jay split the 400. "Double or nothing," the man said again. Jay won two more games, double or nothing each time. In the last game, Big Jim only sank two balls. Jay's pants pockets were bulging with the wadded up bills he had put there. Big Jim had lost a lot of money, more than even he could afford to loose. The next game cost him all of his cash plus a promissory note. Jay wanted to quit, but Jim insisted on going double or nothing again and again, until the man bet his business, that he signed away on a bar napkin, against the big pile of money that he had lost, along with all of the notes that the Russian kept in his top pocket.

Like all people who feel that life owes them something, Jim felt that his number was coming up, and then life would repay him for all of its cruel tricks. The final game of the night ended just as all of the others had, with Jay cleaning the table quickly and Big Jim left standing like a cigar store Indian, wondering what had happened to him. There was nothing left to bet. Jim owed Jay everything, the dealership and all of the money he had in the world. There went braces for the kids, the cabin in the mountains, the color TV, the new furniture. Life. "I, I can't give you the dealership," stammered Jim with his eyes nailed to the floor. Nick pulled the man up by the collar, saying, "It's ours. You lost it fair and now it's ours. If you want, maybe we'll give you a job washing cars," said Nick, mockingly. Meanwhile, Vic stood quietly near the exit with his arms crossed. Jay was more understanding, quietly listening with his angel face in his clean slacks and white button down shirt. "I can't give it to you because I don't own it. It belongs to the bank," Jim said, crying. "You," said Nick, raising the man's head by his shirt collar, ready to hit him before Jay stopped him.

"I guess that these aren't much good either," said Jay, taking the notes from Nick's shirt pocket. The man shook his head and continued to look at the floor, crying. Nick hit Jim in the gut. The man crumpled as the Russian turned to expend the rest of his anger against the wall with a clenched fist. "Stay here, I need to talk to my partner," said Jay to Big Jim, who nodded compliantly. Brother Vic guarded the door, Jay and Nick spoke quietly in the corner, and Jim put his head down and sobbed like a baby.

After a few minutes, Nick approached Jim and

said, "Here's the deal. We keep the cash you lost to us." Jim nodded in agreement, standing tall for the first time since his destruction. "And you give my partner and me each a new Chrysler Imperial." Jim hesitated, and rubbed his chin. "Either that, or...." The Russian slapped a pool cue into the meat of his hand. Two other men guarded the door with Vic, and Jim quickly realized how painful "or" would be. He agreed to the deal. The next day, Jim was paid a visit by the boys. He handled the deal himself, the dealership manager and the entire sales staff gossiping as two kids drove off side by side in showroom new, matching black Chrysler Imperials. There was even more talk at school that Monday morning when Jay showed up, driving a better car than any of the teachers owned. Everybody said that his father had spoiled him rotten.

THE GREAT BIKINII BOYCOTT

After a five hundred year layoff, the women of the world had entered the sea again, only to find that it had become nearly too polluted to surf. Each day enough human waste to fill the Rose Bow,l twice, was being flushed into the Pacific. Added to that were mountains of pet crap and oceans of motor oil, pesticides, and a steady stream from hospital bedpans. Women, who had recently rediscovered that the ocean was their birthright, were not going to sit quietly like Melanoma Barbie, on the beach, as many of their foremothers had done. No. They were going to unite and fight in a way that would wake the men of the world, even Joe Six Pack, who sat comfortably huddled up next to his half dozen cylindrical buddies, awaiting the opening of each of them along with the ceremonies of the Olympic Games.

I don't remember who won what that year, but nobody will ever forget the incident—the most beautiful women in the world, shown via satellite, standing on beaches internationally, not in bikinis, but in Victorian dresses, ankle length muumuus and other skin barricades. The women of Brazil were covered head to toe in bed sheets; some even wore veils to hide their faces. The women of France wore pickle barrels. Women from the United States looked about as sexy as sea slugs in their burlap sacks. And so it went, women everywhere, dressed in ways that kept their bodies hidden, as Six Pack adjusted the focus, hoping to shake himself from the nightmare. The camera turned to Sharon Stone, wearing a lab coat that did not fail to show her curves. She was standing in front of a world map aglow with small, white lights, representing the coastal cities being affected. Even the dullest man in the world realized that something was up. Then Sharon bombarded us with non sexy facts about chemical waste, oil runoff and reservoirs full of recycled brew, fermenting in a tank the size of Lake Michigan, and ready to flow as one vast, toxic golden cocktail, into the sea. Statistics on the cost to public health, and the loss of marine life were astounding, but barely raised the blood pressure of the billion man armchair army. Then came the message, spoken by hidden beauty in French, German, Italian, Portuguese, Spanish, Swiss, and a dozen other languages, as the flags of solidarity, the tiny tops and bottoms usually worn each summer, were waved between thumb and forefinger, to a hungry male population. The message: "We're not putting them on, until an international Clean Ocean bill is signed," came through loud and clear.

The shot was heard around the world. Post game rooting was at an all-time low that night. The world's most successful strip tease had been accomplished in reverse. As you now know, the breweries, clothing companies, surfers, fishermen, musicians, construction workers, sports and skin lovers internationally, raged as an angry sea, demanding a strict Clean Ocean bill. As of last year, the bill had been signed by every "civilized" country in the world. Already the oceans are becoming clean and blue, thriving with numbers of sea life not seen since before the industrial revolution began. People going into the water once again find health, not disease. Women of the world—the dolphin, the starfish and the entire male population of this planet salute you.

CAPTAIN COURAGEOUS

As a member the prestigious Duke Kahanamoku surf team along with Fred Hemmings and Butch Van Artsdalen, it was Paul Strauch's job to keep the Duke from dozing off during press conferences. Duke wore dark glasses to camouflage his napping habit, which he often did at press time. One tap on the knee would wake Duke, and he would answer "yes" to the question. Two taps on the knee brought the answer, "no." Naps were not confined to land, however, and while working as a diver, cleaning boat bottoms in Honolulu Harbor, the father of modern surfing would curl up near a keel and snooze until he ran out of air. His relaxed manner carried over to everything he did, especially fun, which he loved having.

Disneyland had just opened and Duke wanted to be among the first in line for the rides. He loved the Jungle Boat ride best, where animals would appear along the riverboat and the captain would fire blanks from a pistol at them. The little boat was moving along the track, and the brave captain did his duty to protect the passengers by shooting at the hippos and crocodiles that threatened safe passage. A wide-eyed young boy seated next to Duke was taking the trip for the fist time. Duke looked at him, saying, "You'd better hang on, this ride's gonna get rough." The boy held tightly to the rail as the boat hit rapids and the vessel was tossed around violently. As was his lifelong habit, Duke wasted no time in rescuing others. He stood up and took hold of the tiller of the boat and began steering, much as he had done for years in the outriggers off of Waikiki. He was jerked from side to side as the boat teetered on the edge of control. The little boy looked with admiration at Duke, who was hard at work keeping the vessel from going over. The Hawaiian's majestic white hair was flying as he held onto the tiller and the little boy hugged his seat tighter.

Suddenly the water subsided and the boat was moving in calm water again. The captain tied up to the dock, and the little boy approached Duke to thank him for saving him and his entire family. "It's a good thing you listened to me," said Duke, putting a gentle arm on the boy. You gotta be prepared when things get rough."

FRENCH KISS

Dad had spent two thousand dollars on a cabin near Lake Arrowhead, one of dozens of those tank of gas from Los Angeles retreats that lured city dwellers with the promise of swimming and fishing in a basin that had probably been fished out the day after the fishhook was invented. As children we loved playing hide and seek in the clean air and the tall pines. Now, at fourteen years of age, I didn't want to go on vacation with the rest of the family. I wanted to stay home and skateboard the sidewalks of the new mall where hodad girls hung out in white Levis and extra large T-shirts, waiting to be picked up by real surfers like me. I had never picked up a girl before, but believing that I soon would, I told my father that I wasn't going. He told me to get packing. I took my next door neighbor, Benjie, along with me.

At Arrowhead, Benjie and I skateboarded from our cabin to the lake, carrying our fishing poles and jars of salmon eggs. We had made great preparations in order to catch nothing. We got to the lake early, and squatting to skip stones, Benjie told me about a girl he had made out with just a week earlier, saying that they had French kissed. I told him that I had French kissed lots of girls myself, although I had never even put an arm around a girl before who wasn't a relative.

The lake was blue and glassy, and we thought to rent paddleboards and take them out and cast out into deep water in hopes of landing one of the legendary German brown trout we had heard about, but never seen from shore. It would be another half-hour before the paddleboard concession opened up, so I pulled my knife from my pocket and we began a game of stretch. After two throws, my knife pierced the dirt too far away for Benjie to make the stretch and I won the game. Pocketing the knife, I looked up, surprised to see a big yellow school bus rolling down the road followed by two other identical buses. Ben said that we should get first in line for the wooden paddleboards before the crowd got to them.

As we stood there waiting in a line of two, one of the buses passed near enough for us to see the occupants. A window was pulled down and a girl poked her head out, smiling, yelling "hi." Two other girls crowded the window to get a look at us. Then there was a flock of girls, all yelling "hi, hi, hi." The entire bus was filled with girls, all about our age, all, apparently, headed for the lake. We were certain that the next bus would contain equal numbers of boys, but that was wrong. It too was packed with girls. So was the third bus. "There must be two hundred of them, Ben," I said, watching our dream roll by. "Yeah," he said, "and we're the only boys around for miles. We can have our pick!" It was true. There were three busloads of girls and two boys, not counting the guy who was coming down to rent the paddleboards and a couple of dorky lifeguards. This would be the weekend that I learned to make out. Then I became worried. I didn't know how to make out, and I couldn't ask Ben. I had told him that I'd done it lots of times.

We watched the buses roll up the hill, until they parked near a set of cabins just beyond the lake. The paddleboard concession opened, and Ben and I each put down 50 cents to reserve boards for the day. We went to the bathroom, slicked down our hair, stored our fishing poles into a tall locker and waited. At first the girls trickled in, but soon they were pouring in, not worried about swimming or paddling, focused only on us, crowding in like we were movie stars, to ask our names, giggling as we introduced ourselves. Within minutes, Ben had a cute blonde girl with a duck tail on his paddleboard. I watched him stroke out toward the dock in the middle of the lake, laughter everywhere as they grew small in the distance. When Ben intentionally tipped the paddleboard over, the girl screamed and we all looked to see them fighting playfully in the water.

"Take me paddling, please." "No, take me." Two

girls argued and one stood behind them, quiet and shy. There were other girls too, shy bunches of them, a stampeed of pretty faces and young breasts, all wanting to be the one to go to the dock with me, where we would make out. Nervously, I asked the quiet girl, who had dead straight blonde hair, the type that hodad girls wore in those days, to paddle with me. She wore a nice two piece bathing suit, no braces or pimples, blue eyes. Her name was Patty. Patty's plump little friend wanted to come along, but Patty stared her down. The plump one backed away.

As I paddled, trying to keep my balance, the quiet girl dragged her hand in the glassy water and began to speak. "You probably wonder what all these girls are doing here. Well, we're supposed to be on a religious retreat, but all anyone wants to do is make out with boys." She said that she was a freshman at Hollywood High, hated school, hated her parents and was going to run away from home the day she got back there.

I didn't say anything. Patty was doing all the talking, laying in front of me on the board, talking as you would in your room if nobody was there, or the way a girl would write in her diary. "Like I said, I hate my parents. They don't understand me at all. They made me break up with my boyfriend, Ricky, just because they found us making out on the lawn. Oh yeah, and they caught me smoking once or twice, and I had a few drinks at a party, and I stole some gum and a few bucks, well twenty bucks from my mom's purse. Big deal, you know!"

If she knew how to make out, she must have known how to French kiss, and maybe it was the same thing. I wasn't sure. Then I got worried again. She would probably want to French kiss with me when we got to the dock. I slowed down my paddling, and she kept talking. "Gee, you're strong. I can't wait to get out further where I can feel your muscles. You're so quiet and shy. I think that it's cute in a guy, to be quiet and shy. Fabian's quiet and shy. Not that I ever met him or anything, but that's what I read in a magazine once. Hey, you know what? You look like Fabian. Did anyone ever tell you that? A lot of girls think that Elvis is cuter than Fabian, but I think that Fabian's cuter than Elvis. Way, way cuter! Geez! I want to take your picture, not now because I didn't bring my camera, obviously. I mean, where would I put it? Oh gosh, I can't believe I said that. Really, nobody will believe that I made out with a guy that looks just like Fabian. Did you see *Gidget*? I love that movie. You look a lot like Moondoggie, but more like Fabian." The quiet girl kept talking, and I kept paddling, slower all the time, wondering how I was going to make out once we got to the dock.

We were nearly at the first dock where I saw Ben do a flip, showing off for his girl, who's duck tail had flattened out, but she hadn't. Crawling back up the wet steps Ben put his wet arm around the girl and smiled. They both waved and Patty yelled "Hi, you guys." Ben and his girl waved and smiled again. Patty began talking faster and faster.

In less than one hundred feet she had talked about her brother, her friends, her dog, her cat, her hamster, potato chips, her favorite and least favorite subjects in school, how she wanted to get a horse, movies and records, people she knew and didn't know and all things that are boring, unless you want to French kiss with somebody. As I paddled, I tried to remember scenes in the movies where I had seen people making out. The beach scene in *From Here To Eternity* showed a man and a woman moving their mouths quickly back and forth when they kissed on the wet sand. That must have been what French kissing was, moving your mouth around a lot. I paddled faster.

Once at the dock I wanted to stay in the water. There was a bulge in my swimsuit that I didn't want Patty to see. "Think of something else," I said to myself. I thought of The Three Stooges, and everything was fine again. But when I climbed up on the dock, I had to lie down on my stomach so that Patty wouldn't see my bulge. Eyes closed, I reached over to kiss Patty on the lips, but landed instead on her forehead. She pulled away. Oh no. I had done the wrong thing. She wasn't that type of girl. She was a religious girl, a good girl. "I'm so sorry, Patty. I'm really sorry," I said. Patty laughed. "You missed," she said, pursing her lips and waiting for me to press my mouth against hers.

I kissed her long and hard, moving my mouth back and forth like they did in *From Here To Eternity*. Making out was easy and pretty fun. After a long time, Patty pulled away from me and gasped for air. Then she smiled and puckered her lips again. This time, she opened her mouth and when I kissed her she tried to force her tongue down my throat. I gagged and pulled away. I looked at her, thinking that I should paddle her back to shore and find someone with more experience. I could have anyone I wanted from the pack, I figured. I wasn't sure what to do. "Haven't you ever kissed a girl before?" she asked, sitting up and pulling up the straps of her bathing suit top. "Yeah, lots of times," I replied. I wanted to tell her that she was a lousy kisser and that she did it wrong, before going to shore and getting someone else.

I couldn't hurt her feelings, and so I kissed her again and opened my mouth. Her tongue went right in, and she began breathing hard and her hands wandered all over the place. It wasn't really that bad. Suddenly she stopped, put her hands on her lap and said, "We better go back before I get too excited." I had heard of kids having epileptic seizures, and so I said "Okay, okay," making a move toward the paddleboard. Before I could get away, she pulled me from the edge of the dock, right on top of her. There we kissed with our mouths opened, her tongue moving through the inside of my mouth, her teeth biting my lip, saliva dripping grossly while I tried to think of The Three Stooges, who had become powerless over Patty. We lay there for hours, kissing hard and getting sun-burned until someone on the beach with a bullhorn announced that it was time for the girls to have lunch. Sadly, I paddled her to shore. She didn't say a word on the way in, and I concentrated on the Stooges.

As we made shore, I could see the disapproving frowns of camp counselors, all glaring at Patty and me, just like they had at Benjie and Duck tail, moments earlier. On shore was a big table laid out with food that Ben and I were not invited to share. We went to the lockers and took out our peanut butter and jelly sandwiches and ate them alone, on the cold concrete, leaning against our locker. Ben said that he had made out for so long that his lips were rubbed raw. "It looks like you did pretty good, too," he said, examining a red mark on my neck that I later found out was called a hickey. "Yeah," I said. "We made out like crazy." Ben asked me if I had French kissed with Patty. "Not yet," I said, "but I plan to work on it right after lunch." If kissing the way that Patty did was this much fun, I couldn't wait to see what French kissing was like.

THERE GOES THE NEIGHBORHOOD

Some citizens like to boast that they have put their town on the map. Helen, the prize of the tiny Northern California town of Santa Nicolita, is famous there for keeping her town off of it. Because of her, the name of the hamlet that she shares with approximately 8,000 other grateful citizens does not appear on any travel brochures. There are no highway signs screaming out for tourist dollars. No golden arches. No video arcades. No tract homes. No proof other than seeing the place first-hand that Santa Nicolita even exists. And yet, there stands the local hardware store offering everything from nails in oak kegs, to votive candles, to high school yearbooks. The five and dime sells, rents and sometimes loans out everything else. There isn't a convenience store for 60 miles, and the only large chain you'll find is the one that prevents kids from peeling out in Jim Dudley's nut farm. The town escaped death by strip mall because of the courage and creativity of a four foot eleven inch, ninety-two pound pastry chef whose homemade bread is the rage of Humboldt County.

Helen had traveled far enough to have seen the vast desert communities, evergreen woodlands, beach towns and flower fields sprout look-alike plaster boxes all boasting the same faux red roofs and plastic Roman pillars. She had seen Southern California sealed below a moving glacier of costume architecture, Formica countertops and superhighways. Years ago, she had tried to slow the glacier with the cardboard sign that she held in protest of the proposed Diablo Canyon nuclear power plant. She nearly drowned in paperwork and tears, trying to save a eucalyptus grove where millions of butterflies hatched each spring in Santa Barbara. She had seen wild canyons filled, winding rivers straightened, hills leveled and vast new developments arise with ironic names taken from the lake, the river, or the mountain that had been destroyed to create them. She cast a weary eye on the cash and carry yuppies that staked out city blocks in their evil black Beemers. And she watched as the broken-hearted neighborhoods reacted, too late. Punta

Mita, Cabo, La Jolla, Del Mar, Encinitas, Oceanside and San Clemente had nearly been swallowed whole. Then the locusts turned east, mowing down everything from Barstow to Vegas, leaving an open wound all the way to Phoenix. No sooner had they ruined one place then they had their eye on another. "Get away from it all in Colorado." "Enjoy smog free living in Utah." Small town after small town had surrendered to lot busting floor plans that didn't offer a snail enough room to stand on a two-inch row of sweet basil.

When the swarm was sighted in Ventura, some people in Santa Nicolita became alarmed. When tractors began to outnumber artichokes in Watsonville, the best pastry chef in three counties called a meeting that attracted over 1,000 angry citizens. One man came on a tractor, brandishing a loaded shotgun and shouting, "They ain't takin' my farm!" An elderly couple who had been born and raised just out of town made the trip in their Chevy Nova, that they had bought new in 1965 after enjoying a good year raising almonds. Dead heads came out armed with guitars and tambourines, offering to play off key Jerry songs for free. Veterans carried plastic American flags and declared a kind of war against a new enemy. Mothers offered to bake pies. The football team offered to kick some corporate ass. The parish priest offered to say a mass once a month, and fast and pray for two weeks. The prom queen said that she would do whatever it took. Helen was encouraged by all of this, but she knew that it was not enough. The hungry machine at the door wanted their town.

Helen grabbed the microphone, suggesting that someone offer a blanket to the elderly couple shivering on the grass. The ancient PA added static and feedback to her already nervous and cracked voice. "These are drastic times, and they call for drastic measures," she said to the cheering crowd. She then introduced a young man from "Planet Panic," a radical organization that had successfully saved old growth redwoods from becoming new growth condos. The young man politely explained how to spike trees and fill a tractor's gas tank with sugar.

Some cheered wildly, but most of the town's residents were worried that somebody would be hurt, or go to jail.

"We just got to get out and vote," shouted one farmer. "They don't listen to voting, it's gun's talk loudest," said the farmer on the tractor, pointing his shotgun to the sky. "They'll listen if we all go to Sacramento and tell Tom Hayden what's going on," said a petite young woman in a summer dress who could barely be heard above the crowd. "Do you trust politicians to save your town?" shouted another, older woman. "You damned fools; you can't stop progress!" shouted the local realtor. The poor guy was just protecting his livelihood, but that didn't keep him from getting shouted down by a sea of boos, or being tackled by a lineman from the football team. That first meeting broke up in a minor brawl that involved mostly threats and pushing, as the town's citizens sensed their helplessness and turned their rage away from the unseen hand about to clobber them, to each other. The local newspaper called it a riot, but nothing was damaged, except for the realtor's pride and his cell phone, that the football player replaced the next day, along with offering the man an apology. Everybody wanted to move to someplace else in order to avoid watching their homes get plowed under. If they had looked around, they would have realized that there was no place else.

Helen cried as she drove home down the lane of poplars that her grandfather had planted sixty-some years ago. She stopped for two ragged surfers crossing the tracks. They had ridden a lumpy north wind swell that had not dropped below six feet in four days. A boy and his father, who had fished a small creek, walked up the single lane of Main Street with two pan-sized trout for dinner. Lovers kissed behind the local store. A bum tried to negotiate the price of a beer at the local saloon. None of the houses were fancy, but each was different from the next and all displayed the quirky character of the person who had built it. There was the barrel house, the derby house, the castle. Several of the oldest houses in town were constructed entirely of adobe bricks. A 12 room motel built like a ship, called Noah's Ark, featured a different life size stuffed animal in every room. There was a rundown cinema where the elderly owner dressed in a tux each night and escorted each patron to their seat with a flashlight, even though half of his customers were kids who had sneaked in through the bathroom window. Other institutions included Edna's Hair Salon, Champs' Bird Dog'n School and Little Bill's Coffee Barn, where you could bring your own fish and Bill or his wife, Dolly, would cook it for you. Everybody brought their own coffee cup to Little Bill. He personally hung them by their own hook, and you helped yourself to refills whenever you wanted.

Helen envisioned the town dead beneath flat, black streets with perfect sidewalks and those soft yellow streetlights, blotting out the stars on clear nights. There would be a new coffee shop that looked like every other coffee shop in the state, a mile of cars, a nice bookstore and every type of taco, hamburger and pizza you never wanted. She smiled to think that there might also be a library and a fun park for the kids, but where would they put it? on Reb's Trout Farm? Well, at least there would be jobs for everybody, she reasoned. She was at the crest of the hill when she looked down to see the lights of the town turn on as the soft glow of the sun began to fade. "Never," she shouted to nobody.

By midnight, Helen's tears had hardened. By the time the sun came up, she had outlined a simple plan that she called the "Save the Neighborhood Kit." The idea had actually come from a party where a few of them stood in the kitchen and made jokes about doing just such a thing. The following have been taken from Helen's notes:

1) Bury all fish guts in the lot being sold.
2) Get people from Neighborhood Watch to sit amid piles of beer cans, holding signs that say, "Will work for... "
3) Graffiti your own walls if you live near a proposed development. Use a water-based paint that can be scrubbed off when

the developers leave. Phrases like "New Comers Go Home!" are good. The more threatening the message, the better.
4) Buy a cheap but loud stereo and connect it to a motion detector. As soon as anyone sets foot on the property, Marylyn Manson cranks up at full volume.
5) Encourage neighborhood kids to peel rubber on city streets. (The sheriff has agreed not the ticket them).
6) Dump old cars, refrigerators and other junk in or near vacant lots.
7) Follow the example of Texas millionaire, Stanley Marsh, who put up signs reading, "Home Of the World's Largest Poisonous Snake Farm," around the periphery of his property when threatened with development near him.
8) Hang your laundry on a clothesline on weekends.
9) If you need to swear, swear loudly and out of doors.

The next week the community gathered again. Realizing that he had no future among the closed minded, the realtor moved to Sacramento where he took a job as an accountant. Helen's plan was approved without so much as a heated discussion.

Not only did the plan work, it worked so well that some of the town's folk long for the old days when they could watch developers and realtors, trampling over each other to see who could leave town first, their luxury cars mysteriously developing flat tires, bottoming out into sink holes, shaking their well shorn corporate heads, deserting the place with the belief that they had visited the world's largest out patient mental institution.

While there have been very few changes in Santa Nicolita in the past few years, some of its citizens plan on placing a statue of Helen in the park. When asked her opinion of the honor, Helen rolled her eyes and said one word, "Progress."

THE HOLE

I remember being in the Burland Surboard factory and seeing a broken piece of wood on the wall. They said that it was the biggest piece of Carl Ekstrom's board that they could find.
—Skip Frye

In 1947 Towney Cromwell had the inside track on swells. He was working at Scripps' Institute of Oceanography, and he passed the word to his buddies, Bill Isenhouer and Woody Ekstrom, that a massive north swell was coming. The message was more of a warning, really, the waves were expected to be bigger than anything the boys had seen in their lives. The news was received with gladness, and the decision made—La Jolla Cove.

True to the predictions, the surf came up, closing out every spot on the coast except the Cove, where massive lefts peeled into the uneven beach, pinpointing all of their fury on a tiny inlet, a boiling cauldron known as the Hole. Isenhouer paddled out at the inside break, Devil's Slide, while Ekstrom stroked for the main peak where he rode the biggest waves of his life to that point. An outside set darkened the horizon, broke in deep water, and ripped the redwood plank from Woody's steady hands, before driving it to shore, and into the Hole.

The lull lasted long enough for Woody to think that he could swim in and retrieve his board. After clearing the foam away, he began the long swim in. When he spotted the broken board, he began a desperate sprint. He heard it before he saw it. A set rumbling at the point. Soon the entire force of the Pacific would be on him. When the wave came it was worse than anything he had ever experienced. He dove down and hung onto the rocks on the bottom.

Isenhouer was having his own problems from that set. He had lost his board, and as the massive amounts of water ricocheted off of the cliffs surrounding Devil's Slide, they turned the sea into a raging river that was impossible to swim against. He had just enough left to sprint for shore when the lull hit. After struggling against the current for 20 minutes, he collapsed in the sand.

Meanwhile the sets continued to slam the cliffs outside, and Woody treaded water, dodging the pieces of redwood that had once been his surfboard. From the cliff, violent shouts indicated another set coming. It was a big one, and it took a long time for the soup to clear and to see that the teenager was still alive in the Hole. Woody's mother had already received the tragic news. Her son had died during the storm of the century. But the boy was half-alive, fighting for life, and getting too tired to dodge the bombs pouring in. He took a few on the head, surfacing to see his rock sepulcher. Then came another brief lull, and the boy spotted a narrow clearing that led straight to the slippery rocks of shore and nearly certain death when the next swell hit. He had to try. Using all he had left, he stroked hard, fighting his way up onto the rocks as the ocean reared up behind him, and prepared for a final body slam. He was stuck in the inlet with nowhere to go—the next wave would finish him. His greatest hope was that it would be quick and painless. Suddenly, his foot rested on a flat rock. Moving forward, he noticed another one, then, another. Nobody had ever told him that local fishermen had cut out a few rough holds into the rocks. It was just enough to scale the cliff.

Woody stepped forward as the first wave in the set blew up behind him. He was far enough away by then to receive nothing but a good soaking. Slowly, he made his way to the top of the cliff to catch his breath and watch a set of waves tear into the coastline. Before the day was out, huge hunks of precious real estate would be gone, but Woody would be alive to tell his tale. Later that week, he heard from Towney that the Institute had recorded the set waves at the Cove that day at between 32 to 35 feet. When asked for his thoughts on being stuck in the Hole, the teenager smiled and replied, "I was worried that I was going to die a virgin."

FLIPPED OFF

Howard Benedict has retired from his dental practice, but as a waterman, he will always be a legend in our town. As a surfer, he comes to life at places like Todos Santos when large Aleutian swells pound the offshore reefs with waves of ten feet and more. He's also a world-record holding free diver, going long and deep in pursuit of big fish in shark-infested waters. His skill, courage and lung capacity aside, the thing that separates Benedict from the rest of us is that he never misses an opportunity to try something new. Like most surfers in Southern California, Benedict tolerates the average waves and large crowds of his Cardiff home, biding his time until he can break away to some exotic location.

One morning he was out surfing in front of the Cardiff campgrounds. He had taken a small wave to shore, and was ready to paddle out for another one. Then, he spotted something in the shore break that had not been there earlier. He describes it as a whale of about 20 feet long, swimming slowly in the shallow water. Abandoning his board to the sand, Benedict decided to hitch a ride.

Being a blue-water hunter, he was confident that he could hold his breath until the whale made deep water. A flick of the tail and the mammal was off, swimming quickly and easily under the weekend pack of surfers. They were looking and pointing, amazed to see the man who had filled their cavities, gliding beneath them, propelled by the leviathan. People laughed and pointed and put their feet up on their surfboards as Doctor Benedict passed beneath them, getting the ride of his life. Passengers riding or walking the bike path and those driving on the Coast Highway that morning couldn't believe it. Less than one hundred feet west of the Cardiff campground, was a team doing a trick worthy of Sea World. In true surfer style, the whale, which had apparently become tired of the strange amphibious intruder, flipped him off. Literally. Howard didn't take it personally as he swam into shore to get his board and ride waves in the way that human beings usually do.

YOUR CHURCH OR MINE

In 1967 Chris Green was one of Hawaii's top surfers and shapers. Living on Oahu that year, I bought one of his highly revered Buddha Boards, which I rode all over the island before taking it back to the Mainland with me. In California, I underwent several spiritual upheavals, eventually converting to Christianity. When I returned to the Islands in 1969, my first stop was Oahu, to surf and to look up Green, hoping that he would build me a good board for Honolua Bay. But nobody had seen the board builder for some time, so I hacked out my own board from a retired Phil Edwards Model. The desecration caused me no end of grief and fear in the big days of '69, where I broke my board on the first day of the now legendary swell. I was on a mission to find Chris Green.

The surf magazines had done a good job of spraying the collective consciousness with Honolua Bay, and now Maui housing was impossible to find. A ten-dollar flop on the floor of Animal Farm in Lahaina had left me infected and feverish. In my delirium, I drove into the mountains and stumbled upon an empty chapel in the tiny town of Haiku. There was a house connected to a church, and I was told by a caretaker that I could move in without charge, if I wanted to. Iva, the only neighbor to the west, soon became my spiritual teacher, fasting on water for two weeks at a time, living on pure air and the love of God. My next closest neighbor was about half a mile up the hill.

Life was slow and organic. I spent most of my time listening to two-hour reels of Bible tape and developing a huge garden, more of a small farm, that Iva and Taylor, the previous resident at the rectory, had nurtured from seed in the potent volcanic ground. Occasionally, I would drive Iva's car to banana patch, where Morning Star cut stalks of bananas for us and sold us jars of wild honey. Surfing was fading from my life and jaunts to the Bay were becoming less frequent, settling occasionally instead for the lumpy sections of Hookipa Park, just down the street. While visitors were nearly nonexistent, I did sometimes see the monks from the monastery up the hill, wandering down to pick guavas from our beautiful tree lined lane. They were a quiet, pensive group, up by 3:30 a.m. to ring bells, do devotions and meditate. They projected an introverted harmlessness, and were thin from eating sparrow portions of fruit and grain. I sometimes engaged them in conversation about the thing that mattered most to us— Salvation, that I believed came through Grace and they said came from Karma.

After several of these meetings, the group's leader came with them. Chris Green! I had talked with him for quite a while, before I recognized him. He was thinner than the last time I had seen him and I didn't expect to have him appear at the side of the road. When I asked him to shape me a board, he said that he no longer made them. He hadn't ridden a surfboard in the physical realm for some time either, but claimed that he sometimes meditated surf patterns. I told him of my conversion to Christianity. He told me about Krishna. We compared the scriptures, trying to find a common ground. There was some, but on the main issues, we remained divided. I invited Green and other residents of the ashram to attend church in the country with me. They graciously accepted, and five or six of them, including Green, were at my door that Sunday morning. Iva had picked up several homeless people living on the beach, and about a dozen of us rode in two cars, past crystal waterfalls, and lush fields of papayas until we arrived at the old wooden church, tucked into a valley so green that your eyes needed time to quit hurting. Our arrival was greeted by a conservative, Hawaiian congregation.

I don't recall the sermon, but there was a testimony by one woman saying that she had been healed of paralysis. "Praise the Lord." The words rang against the old wooden beams, in pidgin English. Green's group had been praying silently in their own way for a while, when he stood up to speak. He had a book of Hindu scriptures in his hand, and I doubt that I'll ever forget his words. "I feel a lot of love here. I hope that I still feel love after I say what I have to say. We call our Jesus, Krishna, and our Bible we call the Bhagavad Gita." The group broke into a chant for long minutes, before Green and the others sat down again. The congregation was silent, and I couldn't tell if they had been offended. One of the homeless men, who sat near the back of the church, in the row behind me, stood up to speak. He wore long matted hair and a lava-lava, without shoes or shirt, a stark contrast to the suits and ties of the well-shorn Hawaiians. The man compared his life to a boat, saying that he had been drifting, but that Jesus had patched the holes and the sails, and now he was on course. "Praise the Lord." The congregation shouted for joy.

I was hoping that church would conclude without incident when a huge Hawaiian GI on leave from Viet Nam, stood up and came forward to speak. He looked sternly toward our group and said, "I've been fighting a war for two years, and I've returned to see many changes in this place." A group of men, who by the look of them were either the soldier's brothers, or the line of the Dallas Cowboys, turned around and forced eye contact with us. They didn't appear particularly friendly. The Hawaiian continued speaking as my stomach knotted. " I just want to say..." I closed my eyes and prayed. "...I love all of you. Welcome to our church."

Worship filled the room as many stood up to embrace the newcomers with such warmth that many of the homeless were converted on that very morning. Next came a big feast and we ate and drank and played music on the lawn, not driving home until dark. Some of the homeless camped out on the property surrounding the church in Haiku, where they witnessed the goodness of God, through the love of Iva. Within a few months, the tug of surfing returned, and I moved into town with some friends. I never did see Chris Green again, and I have often wondered what he is doing. We were divided in so many ways. One Sunday afternoon, beneath the hot Maui sun, however, we sat in a garden paradise, designed by a Creator for the enjoyment of all people, and we laughed and talked and ate and sang for many hours.

BABY BLUE

"You buy an old Pontiac, Trans Am in America, ship it to Australia, and sell it for ten times what you paid for it. I've done it heaps of times, and made a packet," shouted the Australian at the end of the bar. I bought him another beer, sat down beside him and learned the details of the scam that nearly broke me.

My friend Dan and I were just about to leave for Australia, when we decided to investigate the scam further. We located a copy of the *Sydney Morning Herald* at the local library, and scoured the want ads. The asking price of American "muscle cars" in Australia had not been exaggerated. Even after storage, advertising, customs and shipping, we would double our money.

The ad in the San Diego newspaper read: Muscle car. Midnight blue. 1978 Pontiac Trans Am. T-tops. Craiger Mags. $2,500, or best. The marine, who was about to be shipped out to the Middle East, said that he had babied the machine since he bought it new in Louisiana, 12 years earlier. It looked good, and we decided on a test drive. He introduced himself as Tank. Dan sat shotgun and I rode behind him, buckled up tightly, knowing that Tank wanted to show us what "Baby Blue," as he called the rattletrap, could do. It started at the touch of a button. Tank jerked into first gear, and we were off, pinned to our seats. Second gear sent us flying onto the freeway, headed south. By the time he hit fourth we were running steadily at 85. "Watch me pass this Vette," hollered Tank, turning around to face me. His foot went down and we passed the Vette like a stuffed and mounted swamp gator.

Tank laughed and reached into the glove compartment for a pint of *Ten High*, that he passed to Dan, who refused it. I also gave it a miss, but the marine dumped the final four inches down his throat, before splintering the bottle in the fast lane. "What's the top end?" asked Dan. When Tank opened it up, I felt like the vibration from the car would cause my teeth to fall out. Just shy of 110, Dan said, "Okay, okay, that's good." We rolled out on southbound five at a comfortable 95, the "fuzz buster" signaling cop, which caused him to drop back to 75. We paid $2,100 for her.

We passed a month in the Sydney suburb of Bondi, riding chunky beach breaks, trying to avoid the hazards of city life, and calling customs each morning to see if our cargo had arrived. Nobody could tell us anything, so Dan and I took a cab to the customs office where a man sat, mushrooming beyond his chair, chasing his half dozen glazed doughnuts with equal parts coffee and cream. Engrossed in his gluttony, he didn't look up when we walked in. I laid our paperwork before him, and minutes later he was thumbing through it, soiling the documents with his greasy fingers. He continued eating, without looking up. "We're here to get our car," said Dan. The man dunked and slurped and looked lovingly at his food before holding out his hand, palm up, saying, "Could be in."

"Will you please check?" I asked impatiently. The man sighed, dialed the phone and asked if a car that matched our document number had arrived from America. He hung up and continued eating, paying no attention to us. "Where is our car?" Dan was shouting now. "Check back in a couple of days," replied the man before we walked out.

Two days later, we went through the same routine, still unable to ascertain if the car had arrived, and if the man's repetitious palm-up gesture indicated a bribe. This game lasted for six more weeks, and the Sydney headlines announced an economic downturn. It turned out to be a recession. Within weeks old businesses dried up. Months later, nobody would have any extra money for "luxury cars." Our vehicle was losing value by the day when a friend informed us that the customs man wanted money. We returned to his office, and I reluctantly put a fifty on his desk. He didn't budge as and I piled bills in front of him. Two hundred Australian dollars finally sprung the vehicle.

We found the cars only slightly damaged, broken into, small items removed, apparently by the ship's crew. The value of our cars had fallen by 25 percent since they landed. Although it was illegal to drive them, we cruised through Sydney, tops open, men eyeing us enviously, women smiling seductively. A lot of people inquired, but there were no buyers. The second week was the same, and so we decided to take Baby Blue for a surf trip.

We blasted south of Sydney, and found good waves with fairly thin crowds. At one break we met a young woman who surfed well. Her name was Ginny. She asked for a ride and we crammed her board in next to ours, through the roof. Dan sat in the back seat and Ginny sat next to me. I showed off Baby's speed while she giggled appreciatively. By the end of the drive, she was resting her hand on my shoulder. At the house, Dan wiggled his way out of the back seat and slammed the car door shut. He slept on the floor that night. I got the couch.

Ginny was up early the next morning—knotted hair and resin-splattered jeans, with matching T-shirt. She went to the porch, spat onto the dirt and rolled a cigarette, which she lit and inhaled along with her breakfast of two sugar doughnuts and half a pot of black coffee. Without saying goodbye, she walked to the road, and began hitching to the local surfboard factory, where she worked as a sander. Dan and I drove around until we found some hard-breaking reef waves.

On the way home we picked up a surfer hitching. He introduced himself as Ian, and began asking about our stay at Ginny's house. I wondered how he knew that we had stayed with her.

"You Sepos keep away from her; she's my girl."

"We slept on the floor, Ian," I said. Dan cracked his neck at the memory.

Ian lowered his voice. "She's not really my girl, but I love her. I'm crazy about her. If she asked me to walk across the Nullarbor Plain, I'd start walking." He was tall and would have been considered handsome, if he hadn't been so skinny. Later I learned that he had been a top Sydney model and a semi professional surfer, who had left his home and career in order to be homeless and near to Ginny. He could have had nearly any girl he wanted. Why Ginny?

That evening, Ginny came home covered with fiber-glass dust and new layers of resin on her pants. She rolled two cigarettes and smoked them quietly on the porch, and drank a tall beer before reentering the house. I asked about her day, and she used a string of swear words to explain it, before excusing herself to the shower. She returned to the front room with her hair brushed and wearing a flower print cotton dress. Then I understood why Ginny. She was beautiful with soft golden hair and a melodic voice. When she floated to the kitchen to prepare the evening meal, Dan and I followed her like lap dogs. "We met Ian today," said Dan, who anxiously chopped carrots beside her while she dissected a chicken.

"Poor Ian," she said. "He sits at my window every night, playing that guitar of his, singing songs or reciting poetry for me. He's lost two stone since he came here two months ago. I feel bad that he sleeps in the bush, and doesn't eat right, but he has to get it in his head that I don't love him. I love Andy. He's so big and strong and thoughtful." Andy, as it turned out was a body builder who had taken forth place in a Mister Sydney competition. He was also a karate instructor. He lived in the city, and drove down on weekends to be with her.

Over the next few days, Dan and I competed for Ginny's affection with flowers and dinners, and trinkets that we bought in town. By week's end, we would not only walk the Nullarbor, but swim it, if she asked us to. She was physically beautiful, true, but there was something else, something addicting about her that made you need more of her each second. Dan pried himself away from Ginny and took Baby Blue back to Sydney. I promised to meet him there in a few days. That first night alone with her, we drank too many beers, and sat on the couch in long embraces, her sometimes crying, telling me about Andy, how he really wasn't very nice, but had often hit her, once even breaking her nose. She wanted to get away from him, but had not met a man strong enough to deliver her. The beer was true to its job description, making me feel brave. "He'll never hurt you so long as I'm here, and I won't leave you,

Ginny." When she kissed me, I felt like the strongest man in the world, saying, "I'd fight Goliath if you asked me to."

She pulled away, dreamily saying, " That's funny, Goliath is what they call him down at his studio." I kissed her deeply, trying to prove my devotion.

The next morning Ginny woke me from the couch, and we hitched to Black Rock, finding a moderate swell with deep barrels before the mid-morning crowds moved in and choked us off and we hitched back home. It was Saturday. Andy had gone north for a bodybuilding competition, and so the test of my valor would be postponed for at least another week. It was late December, nearly Christmas. Ginny made gingerbread cookies and decorated the house with colored ribbon, while Ian serenaded her from the porch. He was singing an off-key version of *White Christmas*, but neither Ginny nor I had the heart the tell him to leave.

Ginny was excited to go to the city, where she had arranged to take two aboriginal boys from an orphanage, for the holidays. We took the train to Sydney, and signed the papers in the lobby of the old building, before the two boys, brothers, walked up the hall in identical short pants, polished leather shoes and starched white shirts. They were silent, holding hands, firmly. Mervin was 12. His brother, David, was nine. The four of us took a cab to where Dan was staying. He agreed to let me drive Baby Blue south again, the boys reaching over to honk the horn as I drove to Ginny's house, Mervin turning up the radio, good and loud.

That evening we all walked through the little town. A young couple with two children whispered and crossed the street in order to avoid contact with their continent's original inhabitants. "It's cuz we're black, isn't it Chris?" asked Mervin, looking up at me. Without reply, I took his hand. In the other hand I held onto Ginny. She held onto David. We walked to the car, and I let Mervin sit in my lap and steer, as we drove to get ice cream cones. "Nobody's mean to black people in America, are they Chris," said David, lapping up his ice cream. I told him that everybody in

America loved black people for all they had done for the country, and that black children were treated especially well. He said that someday he would move to America.

Christmas morning found a tape player for both boys with a *Jackson Five* tape wrapped up, under the tree. The boys played it over and over and took turns dancing with Ginny in the front room, everybody laughing, shouting and singing along to the music. After breakfast, we took the boys to the beach and paddled them out on our surfboards. We pushed them into small whitewater waves and they were quick to stand up, laughing and screaming their way to shore. That evening we ate Christmas dinner, and they said prayers, Mervin whacking David on the hand for opening his eyes while the blessing was being said.

It was a quiet ride back to Sydney that night, and we all cried a little at the orphanage door. Ginny and I drove back to her home, her leaning on my shoulder, closing her eyes, crying softly to match the light rain.

The next morning there were good waves to ride, and decorations to remove as I prepared for another difficult goodbye. I was busy cleaning the kitchen while Ginny went to the garden to pull carrots for evening tea. Without warning the door swung open, and a mountain in a tiny tank top and tight, black jeans blocked the entrance. Goliath stood like a Yosemite bear, ready to break into a minivan and devour a cream puff. His eyes were wide, his mouth agape. I walked forward and held out my hand.

"Piss off Yank." Andy slapped my hand away and stomped through the house, searching for Ginny.

"Where is she?"

"Who, Ginny?"

"Don't play games, Sepo. I'll squash you like a bloody bug."

Ginny walked in, cowering slightly as she introduced Andy to me. I reached out to shake his hand again, and he slapped it away again.

"You been playin' house while I'm away?" He was looking at Ginny, but I answered.

" I met Ginny in the surf today, and came over to help her fix a few things around the house."

"I'll bet you fixed things," said Andy, eyeing my suitcase, which lay opened on the couch. He stormed through the house, knocking things over, smashing pottery against walls, and tearing the toothbrush holder from the bathroom wall, after he saw an extra toothbrush in it. He ripped my suitcase in two, and threw my clothes all over the front room.
"It's not what you think, Andy."
"I said piss off, Yank."
"You should leave," whispered Ginny as Andy put an arm around her.

I turned to go, but stopped safely near the door. In his distress, Andy didn't notice me standing there. I was afraid of what he might do, but he simply fell to his knees and pleaded like a child before her. Ginny pulled away from him. There were some restrained words between them, that I could not quite understand. More than an hour passed before Andy walked, head down, to the door. When he lifted his head and saw me standing there, he stuck out his hand and I shook it. "I guess the better man won, mate," he said. "Take good care of her." He was crying.

"Andy," I called, as he walked down the long dirt driveway, toward his comically small Austin. He lifted his head and stood there, sadly. I felt sorry for him, but I didn't know what to say, and he turned again, and kept walking toward his car. When he saw Baby Blue parked in the dirt, he stopped, put a hand on her, and removed it quickly, as if he were touching a hot stove. He bent down and looked at his reflection in the polished rims. He reached in and honked the horn, smiling dumbly. "Mate!" he said, looking at me. He was a little boy standing in line for an amusement park ride.
"You want to go for a ride, Andy?"

"Oh, mate," he replied, apparently having forgotten about the loss of his girl for the moment. Ginny came to the porch and gave me a long, satisfying kiss on the mouth. If Andy noticed, he didn't say anything. I walked out to the car.

Goliath squeezed into the passenger seat, and I drove out of town, into the countryside, opening it up to 90,100,110. He squealed like a little boy taking the first dip of a roller coaster. Once in the country, I changed places with him, and Andy drove cautiously around for an hour or so, joking regularly that the steering wheel was on the wrong side of the car. He drove to the center of the small town and stopped in front of the pub where he gunned the engine. Everyone, including a few women, who were not allowed into the pubs in those days, but were seated in the restaurant next door, came out to see us. One of the women reached into Andy's side of the car, stroked his hair, and pulled back, to get a full view of Baby Blue. Andy gunned it again, and peeled rubber up the road, turning up the street that led to Ginny's. She stood on the front porch like Scarlet O'Hara.

Andy's pain returned at the sight of her, and he sat quietly in the car for a moment, trying to forget Ginny. "Mate, I've got to have her," he said, meaning the car this time. How much?"
"$18,500 Australian."
"Oh, mate, I don't have that kind of Bugs Bunny."
We haggled over the price, and settled on $14,500. Again, he hesitated. "I'll still have to get her converted to right hand drive. That costs a fortune. I don't know mate." "Did I show you this, Andy? It makes you invisible," I said, turning on the fuzz buster. He was giggling as he wrote the check, and blitzed, invisibly, back to Sydney. Later that week, I met Dan in Sydney, and we split our $1,800 profit on Baby Blue. I felt wealthy as I took the train back to Ginny. We were going to be so happy together.

The morning sun streamed through the windows as I ran into the house and took Ginny in my arms, the petrochemical perfume of her stiff, splattered jeans drowning out the smell of strong coffee and cigarettes. Goliath had been vanquished, and I had a pocketful of money. I tasted tobacco as she kissed me, and I kissed her again, longer this time. Gradually, she pulled away from my embrace.

"What is it, Ginny?" I asked, following her into a corner of the front room.

"Nothing, really."

"But Andy's gone, and I've got a little money, and..."

"That's all very nice."

"Aren't you glad? He'll never beat you again."

"He never beat me. He was a gentle giant. You can see that, can't you? I only said that because I didn't want you to getting too close, which you did." She was crying now.

"But we've had so many good times."

"Yes, we did have a few, but things are different now. Now, you're just like everybody else. Just another Yank, and I don't really like Yanks much."

"It was the car that you liked all along?"

Without reply or saying goodbye, she made her way out of the house, to the road, where she would have no trouble hitching to work. I took the afternoon train in the other direction, to Sydney, where I hoped to locate Andy. With his body, my brains and Baby Blue, we could go a long ways.

GAS CHAMBER

By Joe Barca

My parents used to own a house on Hershel Drive near Windansea that everybody called The Hershel Estates. Everybody stayed there at one time or another, and a guy called Willie the Tailor lived downstairs.

We had one of those old gas stoves that you light with a match. The game was to turn on the gas and see how long we could wait before lighting the stove. It was pretty dangerous, and we'd had some pretty big explosions. It always scared the hell out of me. One time, they left the gas running for a really long time and everybody cleared the house except for Ronald Patterson. As I left the house, I watched him light a cigarette and stand there in front of the stove, calmly, just waiting. I had just made it outside when I heard a sound like a thunderclap. Flames were shooting out the kitchen windows. When I went back upstairs, there was Ronald, sitting in a chair with his legs crossed, smoking a cigarette, and having a beer. The explosion was so powerful that it rolled Willie out of bed. There's a knack to doing that sort of thing.

TRAVEL SICKNESS

You don't take a trip. A trip takes you.
    —John Steinbeck

One particular trip, in early November of 1983, took me and didn't let me go until mid December of the same year. It started, like it always does for me, with a gnawing in the gut. Fellow travelers of the spontaneous kind will recognize the symptoms. Suddenly, nothing looks right. Food tastes bad. The waves are too small, too mushy, too crowded, and the gnawing grows until it bores little holes in your soul and you spill out all over the place.

With three consecutive dry runs to Baja in as many months, I decided to head north. I made my decision while glancing back from atop the cliff after an evening session at Swami's that proved too small, too mushy and too crowded, all at once. On my last wave, a newly graduated kook from the local surf school had called me out after he dropped in on me. By five the next morning, I was attempting to find clean air, blowing VW Van exhaust all over I-5. On the roof were a fat nine-six noserider and a lean six-six thruster. Inside were several bags of food, a tattered wetsuit, a backpack crammed with clothes, a Coleman stove and a sleeping bag. I had no map, little money and, for company, nothing but a distant cousin to Steinbeck's Charlie, a black chow named Diego, who proudly rode shotgun.

My journal for the first few days reads: Tuesday: Small, crowded Rincon. Rode one wave solo into the cove. Wednesday: Heavy rain and wind from Cayucos to Santa Cruz. Thursday: Five foot Steamer Lane. Slot. Fun. Friday: City. Three to five. Good sandbars. No crowds. Cold.

After crossing the bridge, I rode the usual unmentionable spots, dodging northern vibes punctuated by the term "Souther." Revisited my old homestead in Eureka, found decent surf at some jetties, and some sizable, too sizable, point surf further north. The gnawing persisted. Through Oregon and Washington, beyond the Strait of Juan de Fuca, riding slow Trestle-style waves with small, barely competent, hateful crowds. Punched further north. Got lost. Hugged the coast and took a muddy logging road to its splintered end. Spent the night in a grove of old growth trees, and understood how some brave souls in these parts have risked their lives to save them. They were friendly giants who covered us with a green canopy, worth more than the thousand tacky look-alike boxes they were destined to become. Woke to the miracle of empty surf on a driftwood-strewn breach. Oh, to pee freely on the tall pines again. Diego and I had found doggie nirvana.

The surf was challenging and cold, hard breaking and closed out. The gnawing had disappeared without my noticing it, a virus now waiting for a new host in the mud somewhere south of Fort Bragg. The gnawing had been replaced by the brisk joy of solitude. True or not, I felt that I was the first to ride here. Journal entry: "Surfing changes when there's nobody watching. All unnecessary movements melt away. A late takeoff, a strong bottom turn and a high-line trim are paramount." Speed thrills. Soul surfing, a hacked phrase in our time, has nothing to do with wetsuit colors, sponsors or the lack of them. Soul surfing involves how it feels rather than how it looks. It reveals itself in the way you ride when nobody's watching. Would anyone do a headstand, a head fake or a spinner if nobody were watching? Talking about it is as foolish as writing about it. Shut up.

And so it went—cold, blissful rain and less than perfect peaks that topped out at three feet overhead. One morning glassy magic appeared. Similar to Blacks with a 1965, make that an 1865 crowd factor. On the beach or hopping down the trail, I experience a freedom long lost in my city-dweller's life. All excess began to disappear in my surfing. I sang some old songs and shouted and played silly games with rocks and sticks on the beach with and without Diego. We peed whenever, wherever we damn well pleased.

I caught a ten-pound steelhead from a creek, gutted it and roasted it whole on a stick in a wood fire. I enjoyed it, but Diego preferred canned meat. We drove into town to buy a few things, shared a steak at a non-chain restaurant and drove back to the homestead beneath light rain made heavier because it bunched up and fell, buckets at a time from the ancient tree limbs. Day followed cold, blissful day, bathtub wrinkles on hands, feet and forehead. Everything smelled of mildew. I was often cold and always happy. Diego chased raccoons and squirrels, and came to appreciate the thick coat that God had given him. We lived in the forest for a week. Then two. After 17 days without seeing another surfer, neither Diego nor I felt a call back to the warm predictability of San Diego. Then, like a desert mirage, a camper van appeared on the rise of the logging road. Surfers! I prayed that they would go away, or that they were not good surfers, or sponsored surfers with cameras on some "discovery" mission that would expose this little spot to a world who had not earned the privilege of being here. Something about the Canadian license plates and the battered surfboards on the roof softened me. Their friendly waves and smiles were impossible to resist, and fear gave way to gladness as I helped them unpack, them laughing at the sight of the "small bear," Diego, as he ran through the trees. They were from Newfoundland, not surfers yet, but keen to try it with the boards they had built in Skinny's garage.

Six foot three, 140 pound Skinny was in his early 20s, with country-style buckteeth, unwashed black hair that stuck to his forehead as if it had been glued there. Devin, his wider, shorter partner, had a naive beard, and stained teeth. It had been his idea to span the gut of the continent in order to find surf. No wonder you hear so many "Newfie" jokes in Canada. They never realized that there were waves only a few miles from their homes, and so they went 3,000 miles out of their way to find some. The boards had been built after a photo in Life Magazine. Both boards were in the six-foot range and about 18 inches wide. Both were asymmetrical, by accident, not design. Both had oatmeal gloss coats, made still more repulsive by the addition of so many colors that the boards turned brown in some areas while in others the colors separated just enough to offer a color swirl. Resin filled in the deep ravines, and the boards weighed in at about 25 pounds each. On the deck of Skinny's board was a crudely painted knife with blood dripping from it. Devin's board featured two hand-prints painted on the deck with the words "Feel the pain," hand scrawled in blood red lacquer. Each board had one fin made of raw, unglassed pine, attached to the stringer by nothing but two wood screws. Leashes were made of yellow nylon rope, deadbolted to the stringers. I had never seen worse surfboards, and the surfers soon proved themselves equal to them, pearling on every wave—the worst surfboards being ridden by the worst surfers of all time. Still, they were happy to wipe out and come up gasping after being dragged for yards by those unforgiving leashes, which chewed through their thick dive suits and cut into their ankles, which in turn led to deepening gashes. These were kids born to hard-ship, not plugged-in electronic slaves rebelling against a world presented to them on a microchip. Whatever it took to become surfers they would do, and surfers they were, in spirit, anyway.

We spent a week together, camping and telling lies and visiting the local pubs. Each day they stayed in the freezing water from just after dawn, until nearly dusk. Neither wind, nor cold, nor rain, nor killer whales de-terred them. Gradually their surfing improved. Skinny was the first to catch a green water wave, an act of sheer courage that matches anything I've seen on the North Shore. Here was a beginner on a steep, overhead peak that he rode straight to shore, yelling like crazy, fists clenched, leaving Devin a bit depressed, but more determined than ever. On the final day of my trip, I looked up from the open van doors to see Devin paddle spastically for a chest-high wave. He made the drop, wobbled to his feet and rode to the bottom before going straight in the soup, yelling for us to watch him, shouting so joyfully that if the sound fell in the forest and nobody heard it, it would be a sin. He wouldn't give up his ride until his fin hit shore and broke off in the sand. Devin found an extra wood screw in the van, and attached the fin again. After surfing, we all celebrated.

The feast consisted of the remainder of the canned food. We didn't know what was going to exit those tins since Diego had chewed the labels from each of them. Stewed tomatoes, yams, peas, fruit cocktail, baby onions and tuna combined with a half bottle of red wine and five warm Moose Head beers made a memorable party. Skinny tried to dress Diego for the occasion in a T-shirt and underwear, and was bitten by the homophobic animal for his trouble. We had no music, so each of us made up a song about Devin's or Skinny's ride, the words and melody about as bad as their surfing and equally entertaining to us. The next day we surfed the dropping swell, after which Devin and Skinny packed up, arguing over who was the better surfer, before leaving for Newfoundland.

The gnawing was gone, and so like all civilized fools, I decided to return to its source, my home. I took the inland route, through lumber towns, until road weariness bid me stop in Ashland, Oregon to visit my friend, Pim. I called her, went by her office and she gave me the key and directions to her home, asking me to meet her there that evening. She lived in a fairytale house nestled alone in a grassy valley at the end of the road. Her driveway was a 200-foot slope that led to a house, a garage and a redwood barn. Outside sat a tall stack of cut firewood with six inches of snow on it. I exited the van and opened the gate. Without warning, I felt a great pressure at my back. The van! I hadn't set the emergency brake! I tried to hold the vehicle on the bank, but it began to slide. I ran to the driver's door and found that I had, out of habit, locked it. Diego sat upright, in the driver's seat and barked nervously as the van picked up speed. With the van gaining momentum, I ran around to the passenger door and pulled hard. I had locked it also. I clutched the door handle and skidded down the muddy slope, until holding on became impossible. Releasing the handle, I watched my vehicle and Diego roll faster and faster toward the barn. Then came the sick sound of crushing metal and breaking wood as the van became one with the barn, and knocked it clear off of it's foundation.

Sitting on Pim's front porch, Diego licked my face, apparently glad that he was unhurt. Snow fell on the ruined barn and van and I dreaded my friend's return. It was then that a familiar gnawing began, and I wondered what sort of surf trip would be required to calm it.

BARREL ROLL

That wave, which never meant anything to anyone but me, rolled in thirty-some years ago. It was nothing but a blown-out, three-foot Newport Beach bump, that nobody wanted because it was so poorly shaped, brown, ugly. And yet, that little wave was one of the most memorable in my life. My goal on the wave was simple—to hang five, a maneuver that about half of my friends had mastered, but that I was having some trouble doing on a regular basis. As the tide rose and the surf deteriorated on an already crappy morning, my friends, Dave and Ron, paddled to shore, and sat, huddled near a fire, watching the four or five of us who remained in the water.

Knowing that they were watching, I ran to the tip on every wave, hanging five or ten in the shore break without getting back (which doesn't really count unless you do a standing island pullout,) before being blasted by the whitewater. I caught an outside set wave, turned and cut-back until it hollowed out near shore. Before the wave barreled, I was distracted by looking to the beach, there seeing my anxious buddies watching me, bored, hoping that this would be the wave that sent me in, so that I could drive them to breakfast. I took two steps to the nose, and planted myself there, disappointed that I wasn't hanging five on my final wave, but desperate not to pearl again. As I hit shallow water, the wave turned hollow. I crouched low, but did not grab the rail. The wave dredged up sand from the bottom, turning the transparent green water to the color of a chocolate milkshake. As the wet cement churned over me, I became weightless. I was being lifted up, and then rolled over. I closed my eyes and waited for the pounding that never came. By the time the soup cleared, I remained connected to my surfboard. My fin was dragging in the sand. It wasn't until later that I realized that I had completed a maneuver that did not yet have a name.

I, an average surfer, had done something that I had never seen or even heard about. A barrel roll in the tube, in 1964! Dave and Ron were running on the hard sand, pointing and laughing in disbelief. It was my job to remain cool. For that split second I had been elevated above all of the other surfers in the water who were content with the mundane pleasures of hanging five.

JOSE OF THE LIGHT

In 1952 my name was Javier Alfonso Santiago Flannagan, but everyone called me Jack. That started when my father decided that we were no longer going to be half-Mexican, because Mexicans were forbidden to buy property in the city of Bell, the Los Angeles suburb where he hoped to purchase a tract home on his GI loan for a dollar down and a promise to pay the remaining $5,999 over the course of a lifetime. Eventually I moved to Bell with my mother, Lupe, renamed Lucy, my sister Jackie and my brothers Richard and David, who did just fine with their already Anglo-sanitized names. Not that it mattered to me. By the time I was old enough to care I was living with my grandfather. He called me Jessie.

I was sent away because the new place was too small, or because I was too big, or because I was twice caught trying to light the baby's crib on fire, or once wearing my sister's prom dress. Then I went to stay in the stick and tar-paper house that belonged to the large piece of land that is now buried beneath the mass of concrete and steel that supports 200,000 cars a day on a blink of freeway known to millions as Interstate 5.

The house was built by the sturdy hands of my grandfather, Jose De La Luz Santiago, a religious man who had been excommunicated by the Catholic Church for committing, and not repenting of, Mortal Sins. Many Mortal Sins, I am told. The excommunication presented a problem to Jose who dearly hoped to taste the blood of the Eucharist again, but so loved adultery, gambling and drunkenness, things that he did not see as sins, that he could not bring himself to repentance. And so, being a devout man, he invented his own religion, a complicated spirituality based upon the Virgin Mary, Jose Cuervo Tequila and the Union Pacific Railroad.

I remember him kneeling at his nightstand, burning incense to the Virgin, a toy train and a tequila bottle. There, at his altar as he called it, he would weep, laugh, pound his fists and scream in a mixture of Spanish and English, while taking bold shots from the bottle. At the memory of his children, he would groan and shout, "Seven daughters and not even one son; why have you cursed me so, *Madre Mia*; I am not a bad man." Finally he would laugh loudly, pull himself from the floor, take one final blast, and walk into the front room to embrace his Apache wife, Soridtha, the woman whom I knew only as Grandma.

Grandma would wander through the house as someone who was lost, dressed all in black like a dark ghost, holding onto her rosary beads that she always kept around her neck while chanting words that were not Hail Marys, and had sounds unknown to everyone, including me. When I was sick, she would finger the beads and chant the strange words over my bed, bringing me whiskey mixed with warm water and wild herbs to drink. She never smiled, and never cut her raven-black hair, which fell perfectly straight, below her waist.

People who knew her from long ago said that she had once spoken and laughed often. But she had quit speaking almost entirely, and she never laughed anymore, not since the Virgin had appeared to her ten years earlier. Now, she stood for hours staring at things that were not there, nodding her head at them and moving her fingers over the black beads, chanting in the strange tongue.

I was seven years old when Grandma died and took the secrets of her magic down to the dirt of Our Lady of Lourdes Cemetery with her. Gone forever was a wisdom as old as the rocks and a power to cure all things less stubborn than death.

When Jose was late coming home, Grandma would drag me through town, forcing me to peer beneath the saloon-type doors, at *Tommy's Place* if times were hard for him, or the *Florentine Gardens* if he had been lucky. We would wander the streets, me stooping to look for Grandpa's brown leather shoes, which looked just like everyone else's brown leather shoes, except for the solitary red dot on the edge of the right heel that

Grandma had put there, for identification purposes.

She made it seem like we were playing a game, rewarding me with candy when I spotted the dot. Then the game ended, and she would burst boldly into the all-male, non-Indian bar to drag the protesting Jose out by the ear. She never said a word, and the men in the bar did not laugh at her as you might think. Nobody dared to look into those black magic eyes, or make a sound until after she had left.

Because of her sorcery, and the seven daughters she bore him, Jose believed that he was under a spell of bad luck. It was the spell that made him lose at poker even when he had three kings. The spell too had caused his chickens to lay eggs so small that he could not sell them to the neighbors for fear of ridicule.

For more than forty years he had tried to break the curse, laboring daily at his shrine, ever since the train had run over his head when he was a young man of twenty. When Grandpa referred to that, the time of his "conversion," as he did at least once a day, he would smile sentimentally, cross himself, and speak about the miracle of the train.

Mother said that he was drunk when he laid down near the railroad tracks, believing in his foggy brain that he was in his own bed. Fortunately he did not use the rail as a pillow, but snuggled up between the ties, in the mud. When the train ran him over, it pushed him deeper into the mud, but not before it had caved in the right side of his skull. For the remainder of his life he had a dented forehead, a joyous disposition, and a religion which centered around the Virgin, because he had been wearing a medal of her around his neck at the time, the train, because it had spared his life, and Jose Cuervo Tequila, because it had caused him to fall right where he did. "A little child's drink like wine," Grandpa would say, " A little child's drink would have taken me one step further, and my poor head would have been crushed like a grape." At the word grape, he would clap his hands together loudly, dust them off and roar with laughter while running his fingers in the crevice of his forehead, touching the dent gently, as if it were a holy relic. The curse aside, he believed himself to be the luckiest man alive.

Jose took me everywhere—to forbidden rooster fights, to China Town where withered old men smoked pipes of opium in dark doorways, and to places where I sat alone in his car and waited beneath hand-painted signs that read "Bed 50 cents," while swirling lights colored the cracked brown leather seats in pretty colors. Sometimes the people on the street would come to see a little boy alone in a car at night. "Jose's boy," someone always said brightly, before offering me candy to eat. Los Angeles was a different city then. A different paradise.

Once when Grandpa was very drunk, he pounded the floor beneath his altar, shouting "Jesse, you must break this curse that is upon me. You must lead a good life, a religious life. Maybe you must become a priest." Soon after that, I was sacrificed to Saint Veronica's Catholic School, the place where boys go to become priests. There, I was Jack Flannagan again.

Veronica's was not so bad, really. The school itself was bad, true enough, but the church that sat in the middle of the schoolyard, a stained glass view of heaven against the black shimmering asphalt desert, was the most beautiful thing I had ever seen. The priests appeared as magicians who could see the word of God float down like a dove. They knew things that nobody else could understand. Someday, I too would be just such a magician, or so I thought.

The words came loudly from Jose's altar. "And what if my son becomes a priest, and there is nobody to carry on the name? What of that *Madre Mia*?" I sat in the front room, watching TV, waiting for nothing, hearing the muffled sound of his cursing and wailing while he beat the very dust from the floor. Finally, he came to me sweating, laughing, and holding the broken little train engine, which had fallen during his devotions. He stood there with the toy in one hand, smiling at me.

In those days I did not yet know how to read the signs of heaven as he called them, and so Jose patiently interpreted them for me, pumping his arms, making little choo-choo noises, saying that the train was my life, and that I would carry a long line of others behind me. A virgin priest cannot do such a thing, he reasoned, but an altar boy, one without Mortal Sin, could. When I became an altar boy, the curse weakened, and Jose prospered at cards, until I made my first mistake.

I was headed straight for puberty, and it was Sister Mary Kathleen's job, duty, to keep me from getting there. Sister Mary Kathleen, "Kate" as we called her, was the Sister Superior at Saint Veronica's. She had always been just a nun to me, but now, for the fist time, I saw the woman hiding behind the stiff black cloth. I would stare at her for hours, trying to imagine what was beneath the habit. One day after school I ditched my bike behind the hedge which surrounded her home, the convent, and I waited silently there for her to finish her work and walk by. I was pressed flat in the dirt, ready to jump out and kiss her and tell her that I loved her, but when I heard her shoes strike the pavement, I became like a dead man, frozen in the leaves and the dirt and the bugs.

Every Friday I went to confession with my class where I told Father Francis my sins, which had been multiplying like rats in a cellar. Then, for the first time, I held back a sin. The new sin, which as yet had no decent name, would not come to the light. And how could I say the bad word to a priest? Would this not be a Mortal Sin? Maybe I would die before I even formed the letter 'f' in the word, and then go straight to hell, where my tongue would burn forever. I stuttered and hinted at the new sin.

Father Francis was an expert at sin, and he knew exactly what I could not say. He spoke with a hard voice. "For the sin of beating a boy with a belt, say one decade of the rosary. For the sin of disobeying your grandfather, say five Hail Marys. For the sin of Lust, say three entire rosaries." He finished as usual, telling me to say my penance, make a good act of contrition and go in peace. As I went, I said the three-rosary word, Lust, to myself over and over, rolling it off of my tongue to taste the sweet darkness in it.

At the communion rail, I knelt with the rest of the class, who came and went after saying their little penance, while I squeezed off countless beads for Lust. Finally, only Sister Kathleen and I were left kneeling there. I still had one full rosary to go when it hit me—she too could be saying rosaries for Lust, and that Lust could be for me! I stared at her, prying into her mind as Jose had taught me to do. If she stared back, she had Lust for me.

His first name was Darryl, and while I don't recall his last name, everybody called him Dagger, because of the switchblade he carried everywhere. Dagger wandered up to the rail. Folding his hands mockingly to heaven, he moved in close and whispered, "Be in front of the church at recess." By the time he had left, Sister Kathleen had returned to her seat and I was left alone.

Dagger and his friend, Tim Clancy, were standing in front of the heavy wooden doors of the church when I arrived. They were giggling lightly as I followed them into the dark and empty building. We moved swiftly down the pale hall, to the bell tower. You had to reach high for the first, slippery rung of the ladder. If you missed, you could get hurt. A fall from the top could kill you. Dagger was up first. Clancy, shaky, was next, then me. It was a hard climb, and I nearly fell onto the cold concrete as my knees shook weakly, and I steadied myself with the words Jose often said, "Be bold." Finally I pulled myself to the top where Clancy waited for me, hunched over with his hand extended to help me into the dusty light of a small room. I walked over to the one window, looking down onto the playground where I could see kids playing kickball. Dagger yanked me away from the window and sat me down saying, "Listen Jack. You got sins, big sins, and so I thought you might want to join our new gang."

"We don't want no Mexicans," said Clancy, interrupting Dagger, who pushed him to the floor and told him to shut up. Dagger looked hard and long at me and then asked, "You ain't no Mexican, are you Jack?"

Does Jack Flannagan sound Mexican? Irish, pure Irish," I said, using the words that my father had taught me to say if anyone questioned me. Dagger slapped me lightly across the face and said, "Okay, you're in Jack." Clancy laughed and repeated the words, "You're in." Then Dagger pushed me dangerously near the crawl hole, laughed and said, "Don't fall off Jack."

"Jack off," said Clancy, and everyone laughed loudly.

Dagger turned his back on us, and pissed on the wall and then pulled something from a loose brick. It was a magazine wrapped around a bottle with rubber bands. When he loosened the bands, the pages fell open to an article titled, "The Girl With the 45" Bosoms."

"Get a load of those 45s," said Dagger, motioning to the woman with a cigarette that he pulled from the pack in his shirt pocket. When Clancy crawled over me, trying to get a better look at the 45s, Dagger slugged him in the arm. Clancy sat back, rubbing his arm, but smiling. The bottle was filled with communion wine, which Dagger had stolen from the church. He uncorked the bottle and drank deeply before passing it to Clancy. A small package made of wax paper had also fallen to the floor. When Dagger opened it, a stack of thin, white wafers fell out. "The sacred hosts!" I shouted, reaching to gather the body of Christ with all that remained of my altar boy piety. Dagger yanked the hosts from my hand after I gathered them. He laid one on top of another, made a little, unholy sandwich and ate it in one mean bite. "*Dominus Vobiscum*," he said, pushing a wafer into my face. I sat back, pulled hard on the cigarette that Dagger had given to me, and inhaled my first in a long line of strong smokes. Dagger smiled. "Eat one, or we're going to throw you down the hole," he said, standing above me, smiling and holding onto a host. I took another dizzy drag from the cigarette, and somewhere in my foggy brain was Jose, warning me to turn away. Another drag and he was gone. I ate the host, shaking, thinking, "This is my body." Dagger slapped me on the back, and Clancy passed the bottle to drink from. It did nothing to me since I was used to sips of tequila with Jose. I smoked and pronounced the name Jack on exhale, trying to forget who I was and what I had done.

As our puberty gained power, it became a stench, an abomination to Sister Kathleen. She stood tall and beautiful before the seventh-grade boys, a pale, soft-faced woman, framed in black and white, courageous against our wall of Lust. Dismissing the girls in the class, she began her lecture, throwing all of her goodness against our sins, like a Dutch boy with one finger in a dangerous place.

That night at dinner, Jose asked me if I enjoyed school. I shrugged my shoulders without looking up. "And what is the matter, Jesse, aren't there no pretty girls in your class?" he asked with his usual big laugh.

"My name is Jack!" I snapped to Grandpa. I never saw it coming, but his big open hand fell down on the side of my face with such force that I tumbled from my chair, onto the floor.

"Get up, Jesse," he said without anger in his voice. "Finish your food *mijo*." I sat at the table and finished my tacos in silence.

That night I dreamed that Sister Mary Kathleen was giving us a lecture. Suddenly, she was topless, with the body of the girl with the 45" bosoms. Topless, she danced for us in thin, white panties, punctuating the air with her index finger, sternly warning me, "Do not let me catch you with any girls after school, or I'll give you a real doll to play with." Then she held my face in her soft hands and kissed me deeply on the lips. After pulling away, she threw back her head, laughing and spinning, dancing while the rest of the boys sat on the floor with their hands in their laps.

The next day after school, I volunteered to help Kate clean up her office. That evening, I found Dagger seated on his bike, waiting for me by the bike rack. He grabbed me by the sweater and said that I had broken gang rules by helping a teacher. I pushed him away, and he fell, with his bike, onto the pavement. As I peddled away, he yelled for me to stop, but I kept going all the way home.

That evening at dinner, Jose again asked about girls.

"Yes, Papa, there is one," I said shyly.

"Please to tell me about her, my son," he said, pounding the wooden table happily, straightening up, and leaning forward to listen.

Then I told him all about Kate, even the dream where she had stripped for me. He smiled as he listened, laughing in places. "And did she take off all of her clothes, even the panties?" he asked leaning further forward. "No, just the top," I replied, as he leaned back and his smile weakened. He laughed again and said, "It is okay, Jesse. And, who is this Kate who dances for all of the boys in dreams?"

"Kate is Sister Mary Kathleen, the principal of our school," I told him. For a moment he sat quietly. Then his mouth formed words without making a sound. "A sister." Next he said the words quietly. Then, louder, he said, "A sister. And not only a sister, but the very highest of all of the sisters!" His voice was like a train now. "You must be bold, but not with the sisters; never with the sisters, my son, you idiot son of mine."

He continued yelling and I covered my ears and lowered my head as he stomped his feet and shouted, "My son, the curse will never be lifted if you follow this path. Do not do this to me!" Jose stormed out of the room, to his altar where I heard him praying, shouting, drinking, slamming and breaking things, even after I went to bed where I again dreamed of Kate, this time just the two of us, alone, me rowing a boat on a lake, while she sat topless and the evening sun fell on her perfect body.

Although I respected Jose, I spent every day after school from then on with Kate. In time I discovered her more fully. She had long, thin, white fingers that moved smoothly and accurately making words unnecessary. Her emerald voice made each phrase a song. Her face was that of a happy angel. She had a wonderful wit, and a magical laugh. Sometimes she would play the records of Handel, shutting her eyes, breathing hard, telling me with a quake in her voice, about his writing *Messiah* for God in three weeks with little food or sleep, in a fit of passion. Passion. She knew it. I could hear it in her voice, and feel it whenever she touched me.

In time we developed our own language that was part English, part Latin, part nonsense and love. One day I asked her, shielding my feelings with the new language, about the men in her life. Stroking my hair gently she said, "Jack, I am married to God, and can have no other."

Her eyes were sadly true as mine filled with tears. She reached for my hand and I pulled away, running from her, to the church where I knelt at the communion rail, praying out loud and crying bitterly. The only light came from the rows of white candles burning for the Virgin. I stood before her, put a dime into the box, lit a candle and went back to praying, hoping to soften the heart and bend the arm of the Heavenly Mother. When I felt nothing, I knew that I had fallen from her hand. I confessed all of my sins, starting with the betrayal of Jose. I put my remaining fifty cents into the box and lit five more candles. Surely such a flame would burn Lust and unholy love from my soul.

A sharp, rusty sound along with a thin shaft of light penetrated the darkness as a sliver of illumination fell onto the large marble crucifix that hung, dead center, behind the altar. I did not turn around when I heard the boy's shoes moving angrily toward the rail. I fought against the dark power approaching, trying to see past it, all the way to salvation. A pair of strong hands seized my neck, and I turned to see Dagger. When I gave no resistance to his choking hand, he relaxed his hold.

I ran from the church, mounted my bike and rode with him close at my back wheel, all the way to my front door, where I ran inside to see Jose, looking out the front-room window, hoping to find something good outside. He sat in silence for a long time, not noticing Dagger, who taunted me with rocks and foul words from the street. Grandpa was staring at nothing. When Dagger finally left, Grandpa was quiet for a long time. When he finally spoke, he said that he had lost our house in a card game, to Julio, the man he always called, "The Shark." Because of Julio's bad reputation and because of the way that my grandfather spoke, I knew that Julio had cheated in the game.

For weeks Grandpa was silent in the house, sleeping late and walking around in his pajamas silently during the day. I did not go back to school, but was taken each day to Santa Monica by my uncle Nacho, a surfer who rode the waves there with some other men. Nacho went with me to the shed and together we carried Grandpa's heavy redwood surfboard to his truck. The board had been a gift from a man that Grandpa called Mister Freeth. He had gone to Redondo Beach, back in 1909 to see a Hawaiian ride the first waves in all of Southern California. Grandpa himself tried surfing a few times, but soon gave it up because of the cold water.

Surfing on the heavy board was not easy for me, but soon I could catch a small wave and ride it to shore. Sometimes Nacho would rent a room for us on the beach, and we would stay in Santa Monica surfing and fishing for three or four days at a time. These were good times for me, but I was worried about Jose, and I asked Nacho to take me home to be with him.

Even before I entered the house, I could hear Grandpa at his altar, shouting and drinking. He was there for a long time when he suddenly became quiet. Then there was more shouting and finally loud laughing. Jose returned to the front room still laughing, twirling the ace of spades between his thumb and index finger. "Everything will be okay, *mijo*, The Lady has given me permission to use the magic aces against Julio. Believe it, this was the first card that I took from the deck after I prayed to her," he said, holding the ace of spades high above his head. "But keep a close eye that I do not use this trick on nobody but Julio. If I do, Our Lady has said that the curse will become double. Then I will have 14 new babies, all crying and wetting at the same time. We will surely have poverty also, for the cards will turn against me always, and there will be no eggs from the chickens, or they will be as tiny as the eggs of sparrows." When I agreed to watch Jose, he smiled happily.

Julio matched the black night by wearing a big, black hat and a black suit with silver buttons. The other men— my uncle Nacho, who came in with sand on his feet after a day of surfing, Joaquin, Guillermo and Blind Willie, Papa's Negro friend, all came along too. They were not there to play cards, but to watch the game, to make sure that nobody cheated and that the loser paid up. Grandpa's anger burned deeply when Julio refused a drink of tequila that he had poured for him. The others passed the bottle in silence as the cards were dealt from a new deck.

The first game was Black Jack. After they went through the deck, Grandpa was down by about twenty dollars. Julio was talking big when Nacho went for his guitar to play and sing, to quiet the evil spirits in the cards and not to have to listen to Julio anymore. The next game was high-low, and Grandpa won back his twenty, plus another five. The guitar playing had worked, and Nacho and Julio were quiet now.

Grandpa shut his eyes and prayed silently. I too prayed a prayer. "God, don't let Julio take our house." Grandpa opened his eyes, poured himself another shot and passed the bottle. The game went to five-card stud, his game.

"Come on, Papa," I said, quietly. Julio looked at me with anger. Again I prayed, Father forgive me, for Julio to lose all of his money. I opened my eyes and nodded to him, smiling confidently. His mouth remained tight and turned down in an angry scowl.

Grandpa dropped a card in misdeal, something I

had never seen him do before. He slurred an apology. Julio took the money on the table and demanded a new deck of cards. It was produced quickly, still in the paper wrapper. When Grandpa went for the bottle again, I grabbed it from him. Everyone was silent, fearful at my defiance against Jose as he wrenched the bottle easily from my hand and poured himself another drink. My greatest hope was that a tree would fall onto a power line, causing the electricity to go out as it had last month. No such luck.

Grandpa rocked back in his chair, nearly tumbling from it. He recovered, laughed, took another drink and Julio gave him his cards, which Grandpa laughed at. Julio saw Jose's eyes, and the intoxicated, dare I say it, the stupid look on my grandfather's face.

"How many cards?" asked Julio. Grandpa did not react for a moment, but fumbled with the cards in his hand.

"How many cards?" repeated Julio, forcefully this time.

"Four cards," said Grandpa, in a stumbling, sluggish manner, which made me ashamed.

Julio dealt the four cards to Grandpa, and then took two cards for himself, something that proved that he had at least three of a kind. Grandpa did not seem to notice what was going on, and I prayed, "Three of a kind is a good hand, *Madre Mia*. Please let the tree fall." There was no tree.

The betting began at twenty dollars and Jose recklessly threw down fifty more, a sum which Julio gladly matched. "I'll see that and go..." Grandpa laid his cards face-down and went for his wallet which held all of our money. The wallet fell from his old, wrinkled hand, onto the floor. Trembling, I picked it up and gave it back to him. He looked at me with dead eyes. Straightening up again, he said, "Okay, I will bet you this beautiful house ..." He pulled the thick stack of hundreds from his wallet, and put them all into a messy pile in the middle of the table. Julio's slight smile turned back into a frown. He knew that he had something good, but he also knew that Jose was the greatest card player in the entire city, and that he rarely lost more than a few times in a night. Still, Grandpa was drunk and betting in the dark. Julio hesitated and shifted in his chair without saying anything.

Grandpa reached into his top pocket and pulled out another hundred. He kissed the last of our money goodbye and laid it on top of the pile, waving goodbye to the money like a silly child. Julio matched the hundred. "Okay, this is it, Shark," said Jose, laughing from the side of his mouth. Julio nodded without expression.

Nacho reached down and quickly counted the bills. With astonishment in his eyes, he looked around the room. "Over three thousand!" he said. Everyone fell silent, except for Willie, who said, "Holy Mother of God," and crossed himself in support of Grandpa.

Julio pushed Nacho's hands away from the money, and nodded, this time seriously to Grandpa. "You'd better have something good, old man," he said.

"Call," said Grandpa, slurring the word, and running his finger sloppily over the rim of his glass. "Now, what have you got, Shark?"

"Try four jacks, *pinche' viejo*," said Julio, showing the cards with a burst of sudden joy that nobody shared. The weight of the good hand fell upon us and the room went silent. Grandpa looked at Julio and then, for the very first time, to his own cards with a surprised face, as if the cards were flying cows. He looked like he was going to cry as he rested his head in his hands and then laid his head down on the table. He was drunk, too drunk to move. Why had he done such a thing, when everything depended on this one hand?

Julio straightened up in his chair, flashed a cruel smile at me, and reached out both hands to gather in the pile. Grandpa lifted his head slowly, soberly, and then flicked his cards over. With one turn of the finger the cards fell, fanning out in a perfect row to show four kings. There was silence for a long time, and then the entire room filled up with holy joy. Blind Willie called it a miracle. Nacho kept saying, "I can't believe it. I can't believe it." Grandpa laughed so hard that he blew some of the money from the table. I hung onto his bull neck tightly, as if I would never let go. The house was saved.

It was Grandpa's night, but he did not want the entire thing to himself. He would soon celebrate hard, harder than anyone else, but he could not be perfectly happy while someone in his house was sad. That someone, of course, was Julio, who sat as still as a wooden Indian, still staring at the powerful Jacks that had let him down. I think that I was the only one who saw Grandpa, with his fast, magic hands, palm a short stack of hundreds, and, without anyone but me and Julio knowing it, stuffing them into his opponent's pocket before kissing him gently on the cheek and asking him to share a drink with him, which the defeated man humbly accepted this time.

Before the night was over, Joaquin was sleeping on the couch beneath the mountain of Jose's overcoat. Jose and Guillermo danced cheek to cheek, smoking hand-rolled cigarettes, stumbling over cans and bottles as they waltzed on the front room rug, playing *Corrido De Juan Villereal*, a song about the Mexican Revolution, over and over on the record player. Blind Willie played along on his harmonica and Nacho on his accordion. Julio sat alone in the corner drinking, crying and singing his own sad song. I wondered if Grandpa had used the magic aces to save the house until I realized that he was not even dealing on the last hand and that the deck was a new one. It truly was a miracle.

When summer came again, Nacho took me surfing on a balsa wood surfboard that a man named Velzy had made for him. I met many great and wonderful people including a man who called himself Tubesteak, of all things. Surfing was easy on the new surfboards, but I soon lost interest in it in favor of playing in the neighborhood with my friends.

School started again, and it was in September that I found myself pedaling home on my bicycle and stopping as I often did at Paco's Liquor Store for an RC Cola and a pack of baseball cards. I stood shaking each of the gum-scented packs, thinking, "Okay, if Paco looks at me and says, "What do you think this is, a library?" that will be a sign that Wally Moon, the one player I needed to have all of the Dodgers, is in the pack I am holding. If he says nothing, Moon will be in the next pack.

Paco was busy with paperwork, so I kept trying different methods of divining where Moon was located. Then I heard the click of a kickstand, and looked to see Dagger parking his bike next to mine. Tall and unafraid, he stood there, looking straight at me with a frozen face, for a long time. "Be bold," I said to myself, trying to remain steady. I kept my eyes riveted on him as he pulled out the pearl-handled knife he had been nicknamed for and pushed the button to show a thin, shiny blade. After making a stabbing motion at me with the knife, he bent down and pressed the tip of the blade into my back tire. I was sick to hear the whistling of the air as it left my bike. He stood there for a long time, watching like a cat in the grass waiting for a bird, while I, the bird, waited to die. Paco never took his eyes off of the books he was writing in, except to ring up something for a customer once in a while.

It was black outside when Paco flicked on the yellow light to reveal his sign and Dagger still standing, waiting for me to leave. I thought about running out the back door, but he would get me in the alley. He kicked my bike onto the sidewalk, and stood there, smoking and looking in, waiting for me to come out and to die. After another long time, I walked up and asked Paco to use his telephone. Without looking up, he slid the phone over the counter to me. I called Jose.

Grandpa pulled up in his Chevy, dressed as he always was—gray felt hat, creased khaki pants, flannel shirt buttoned to the top, and suspenders. He looked old and dried up until he got out of the car and came to his full height. Dagger blocked the front door to the liquor store and puffed out his chest at Grandpa. Jose stopped and blew smoke from his cigarette, into the boy's face. Dagger then put his hand into his pocket, no doubt ready to pull his knife if things got rough. Jose flicked his smoke into the gutter and put a hand into his own pocket, touching the straight razor that he kept there for things other than shaving. Dagger looked small to me as Grandpa stared him down. To Jose he was nothing but a little insect that had invaded his land. Compared to a train, he was nothing at all.

Grandpa's laugh filled the store, and Paco looked up from his books for the first time, to see what was going on outside of his place. Jose pulled his hand from his pocket, empty, and reached over to mess up Dagger's perfect and greasy hair. If Dagger went for his knife, I would run out and face the blade myself. Nothing happened. The boy's face froze, as Jose stood high above him, laughing hard. Grandpa wiped the grease from Dagger's hair onto the insect's shirt, pushed him aside and walked into where I was standing by the baseball cards. Without a word, he took the entire box of cards, along with the RC, to the counter.

"Good evening, Jose," said Paco reverently, as he reached back and automatically took a carton of Lucky Strikes and a bottle of Cuervo from a shelf behind him, placing them on the counter. Jose nodded to Paco and paid for everything with a crisp hundred-dollar bill.

He was old, and he went from the store with a limp. But he had a power that fell over Dagger like the shadow of a black panther as we walked by. Jose picked up my bike with one arm and loaded it into the trunk of the car. He was already behind the wheel when Dagger looked at me and mouthed the words, "You're dead, Jack."

"My name's Jesse," I said, before getting into the car and slamming the door.

On the way home, Grandpa opened the bottle, took a drink and laughed loudly. Then he told the story to nobody, to the air, to the holy and evil spirits crowding the car. It was a story that I knew well, the miracle of the train. Although I had heard it every day of my life, I listened to each word in silence. After all, he was my grandfather.

Jose of the Light *is a condensed version of an upcoming novel by Chris Ahrens titled* The Miracle of The Train.

I THINK I CAN, I THINK I CAN

Vickey Tuten was a good girl. Ambitious, curious, fun loving. A seventeen-year old surfer from Belmont Shores, she would carry her board to the jetty and paddle to Ray Bay, that stingray infested river mouth where she met friends, like U.S. Surfing Champion Jack Haley. Noting her intelligence and honesty, Haley gave the girl a job, and she was soon managing the champ's shop in Seal Beach. When Haley and his team took surf trips, it was usually by car. Only once did they decide upon a different mode of transportation.

It was a hot summer day with a clean south swell running, when Captain Jack decided to make a Trestle run, something that required enough stealth to beat the Marines at their own game. Along with Eddie Brenner, Wallpaper, Ernie Morgan, Toes, and one of Long Beach Surf Club's founders, Vickey Tuten, the crew made their way through the Cotton's Estate, past the barbed wire, past the Point, and Upper's, to Lower Trestles, just in time to watch solid six-foot lines turn to onshore mush as the afternoon wind began to howl. Maybe San Onofre would hold the wind.

It was a long and risky walk through enemy territory. They would have to lie low in order to avoid capture. The train engine stood empty, and five surfers climbed aboard. The engineer must have been in the bushes, pissing. Also doing what came naturally, Haley fiddled with the controls and got the big machine started. Boards were loaded, and team Haley moved south. Destination, about a half-mile away, to San O'. The wind had blown out Old Man's. Maybe Mile Zero. Why not Oceanside?

And so the little engine began picking up steam, Haley at the helm, charging through Oceanside, Carlsbad and Del Mar, where residents expressed shock to be mooned by the engineer and his four unruly conductors. Might as well check out Mexico.

Like most surfers, they knew how to start things, but not how to stop them, and the train rattled and rolled, until it ran out of fuel, on the wrong side of the border. Both Federales and Marines wanted the *gringos*, but the USMC yielded to Mexican officials, and the team was treated to all of the comforts of the Tijuana jail. Colonel Tuten, Vickey's father, was able to pull a few strings and spring his daughter and the rest of the crew.

Vickey Tuten Mobley is the co-owner of the Surf Ski Shop, along with her husband Richard. They split most of their time between LA's South Bay and Mammoth Mountain. They drive cars to their destinations.

AIR

If you look at the photographs of the time before the end, you may notice that we smiled a lot. And why wouldn't we smile? Each person lived like a monarch, with enough clothing to keep entire kingdoms warm, and so much food that we paid people to teach us how not to eat it. What we ate was soft, mashed and bland, not resembling anything that comes from the ground today. We never saw the farm that it came from, only the metallic containers that were ripped open by pushbutton machines. So, we dressed well, pushed buttons, ate, and smiled a lot.

I was among the lucky ones—one of fewer than 400 in my district to make it here, to the Oxygen Chamber, before the end, a time that our resident historian calls "The Great Suffocation." If there is ample oxygen in the future, you may understand. We could not. With increased oxygen rations, it's becoming increasingly clear. We had gone insane, one brain cell, one dead tree at a time.

One of my last memories from that time is of reading something that we called a bumper sticker. To understand bumper stickers, you must first understand cars. The car was a primitive machine made mostly of metal, which moved people from place to place. Cars were noisy and took up a lot of room. Every person had at least one car. Some cars made angry sounds, if someone other than the owner came near them. Worst of all, cars burned a toxic substance called gasoline. Gasoline is made from a black sticky liquid called oil. Oil was considered so precious that many people died because of it. When a car burns gasoline, smoke goes into the air and there is less oxygen to breathe. Even though gasoline became more expensive than water, everyone continued to burn gasoline in their' cars. Some cars were decorated with sayings that expressed joy or rage. Mostly they expressed no emotion whatsoever. These decorations were bumper stickers. Since our brains were growing soft and we were losing the ability to speak to one another without screaming, we paid people to write simple messages on bumper stickers for us. Some of the most popular messages were: "Have a nice day." "If this cars rockin', don't bother knockin', " and "I saw Elvis; he told me that he's still dead."

A person with an oxygen-starved brain may display one or more of the following symptoms:
• An uncontrollable desire to stockpile shoes.
• A need to watch families tell their' secrets on an electronic device called television.
• A spastic jerking of the arms and neck, followed by wild cheering when some highly paid man in a uniform runs with a ball, puts a ball through a hoop, or sends a ball into a cup with a stick.
• Sadness or anger when someone misses a ball with a stick, drops a ball or sends it into the trees.

When an entire society has been affected by oxygen deprivation, you may notice these symptoms:
• Machines will dominate work, entertainment and personal relationships.
• People will lust for faster machines, even before the old ones wear out.
• People will move fast and go nowhere.
• How you look will become more important than how you think or feel.
• People will spend a great deal of time locating some of the last remaining quiet places on earth and advertise them on bumper stickers, hats and T-shirts.
• Green paper bearing the likeness of a dead king will be more important than anything else, including friends and families.
• Human waste will be dumped into the ocean.

It's getting late. My oxygen valve has been turned down and I am, no doubt, babbling like some foolish air famished man from the early 21st century. I must stop now before I become too stupid to write. If you are able to understand this letter, please don't make the same mistakes that we of the past century have made. Protect your air at all costs. Breathe. Think. Breathe. Breathe.

AKIDIO

I had been logging time in the Santa Cruz ghetto, turning moldy in a place that would have given Dickens the creeps, trying to stay one step ahead of the "Troll Patrol," a group of misdirected kids who had just been accused of shooting a homeless man with a homemade bazooka. Two steps ahead of the Hell's Angel who wanted Cisco, the Doberman that my next door neighbor had stolen from the pound and left with me, to fight the Angel's pit bull, Diablo, to the death. Either that or I take his counter offer, a fight to the death between him and me. It seemed like a pretty good time to go on vacation. Someplace warm and free of charge would be nice. And so my roommate, Bob, and I decided to go south, back home to Encinitas until some things warmed up and dried out, and some other things cooled down. I called Laurie and Shirley, old friends who said that we could hang at their place for a while.

Just out of Santa Cruz lies a little truck stop with cheap gas and good food. Bob wanted to stop there for fried clams. He put in his order, specifying that the clams be brought to him without French fries. When the order came, however, there were fries on the plate, and Bob nearly barfed seeing them. He was, no doubt, reliving some foul memory. Bob mentioned the fries to the waitress. She smiled, picked up his plate, and gently pushed it across the stainless steel counter that served as a barrier between waitress and cook. "Lou, no fries," she said. Without looking at the plate, Lou pushed it gently back to the waitress' side of the counter. The waitress nudged the plate back to the cook repeating, "Lou, no fries." Lou's smile broadened as he silently lobbed the plate back across the court. The waitress had a powerful return, however, and rallied back to Lou, this time shouting. "Lou, no fries!" Lou returned the plate and, Bob, who by now was salivating, said, "It's okay, I'll just eat around the fries." The waitress and the cook, however, were locked in a battle of wills.

"Lou!" shouted the waitress. "Lou. Lou-u-u-u!" Lou didn't bother turning around. "Damn you Lou, no fries!" Sensing game, set, match, Lou's thin smile broadened and he returned the slam, back across the court. Bob, who could nearly reach his plate, stood to claim his food, but the waitress shoved him back into his seat. "Please give me my order. I don't care about the fries," begged Bob. By now the waitress wasn't interested in anything but revenge against Lou. When she picked up the plate you could almost hear Bob's mouth dripping. But she didn't bring the plate to Bob, as he had hoped. Instead, she called Lou's name so loudly that everyone in the joint ceased conversation and looked at her and the plate that she held in her hefty hand like a shot put. "Lou, you bastard, I told you, no fries!" Lou turned slowly, like a street brawler hit by a punch that would level most men. The cook laughed disdainfully at his opponent, his mouth so wide that you could see his nicotine-stained, rotten teeth and gold fillings. It was then that the waitress launched the plate, fries and all, at Lou.

Lou, who had no answer to the assault, retreated to the restroom to spot clean his uniform while the waitress returned to Bob, saying as if he had just walked in, "What can I get for you"? Bob smiled weakly and said, "I'll take a salad."

The surf in Encinitas was flat when we arrived at Laurie and Shirley's, and it was mutually decided that the four of us would go to Mexico for the day. There, we bought firecrackers, pottery and a souvenir half-pint bottle of mescal. That night we stayed up late watching Johnny and Ed, laughing and talking until about 2:00 in the morning. Suddenly, there was a knock at the door. I answered and found two guys, both with blow-dried hair, tight, polyester pants and half-buttoned rayon shirts. One of them wore a gold medallion. They walked into the house and over to the couch, to sit near the girls, who pulled away, and asked them to leave.

Bob whispered to me that he would handle the situation, and I sat, watching a master at work. "Is there anything to drink in this dump?" asked Medallion. "Only a bottle of mescal, but it's pretty strong," answered Bob. "Get it," said Medallion. Bob held the bottle up and Medallion wrenched it from his hand, saying, "Give me that." Medallion unscrewed the top and began a heroic death chug, which lasted until the bottle was nearly empty. Bob watched as the red worm hit terminal velocity and slipped into the whirlpool before it went down Medallion's throat. Medallion threw the bottle onto the floor triumphantly, and Bob gasped, saying, "I've never seen anything like it in my life." Medallion pushed Bob aside and made a move for the couch and Laurie. Bob was right behind him. "That was fantastic, you drank the whole bottle. And the worm." Medallion was slouched proudly on the couch and Bob was seated right beside him. "Did you know that those Mexican worms don't really die. Nope. They're like sea monkeys, you know brine shrimp. Only instead of coming to life in water, the worms don't wiggle again until they hit something with a carbohydrate base. What did you have for dinner? Was it macaroni and cheese? Noodles would bring them back to life, so would rice, corn or flour. You must have had one of those for dinner. You drank the worm, man. I've never seen anyone do that before."
"Shut up," demanded Medallion.

Bob continued. "By now that worm is swimming through your intestines amid all that macaroni and cheese. Maybe it was a female. Hey, maybe it was a pregnant female. Congratulations, you're gonna' be a Daddy!"
"Shut up."
"Okay, but I think we should celebrate."

Bob went to the kitchen and returned with a beer for himself and one for Medallion. I've got to give him credit. I mean, the guy nearly downed the beer in one gulp. At first it was just a loud burp. Then he turned a pale shade of green and put his hand delicately over his mouth. Then you could see pink goo oozing through his fingers.

Then he let go, not with a polite little Technicolor yawn, but barf the way that Paul Bunyan might barf, violent barf that came from down deep and traveled far—all over the tile floor, painting everything in yellow and pink slop. The girls were furious, but Bob was happy. He even volunteered to clean up Medallion's mess. Instead of a mop, however, Bob returned from the kitchen with a spatula. Then, he began picking through Medallion's recycled dinner, looking closely at the big chunks. Finally, with disappointment in his eyes, Bob looked to Medallion and said, "I don't see the worm anywhere." Medallion began to heave again, but before he could bring anything up, his friend took him by the arm and out the door, which they slammed behind them. "I wish he would have at least said goodbye," said Bob, sitting on the couch, sipping the remainder of his beer, surrounded by Medallion's mess. "We were just getting to be friends."

WORLD WITHOUT PROZAC

Al saw the set wave, heard the horn blow, swung around and caught an irresistible five-foot wall that he destroyed with a series of hard bottom turns and off-the-top combinations. It was the wave of the day, both days, but because he had ridden it, he was given last in his final heat, instead of first, which anyone with eyes could have seen he deserved. On the beach, he took perverse pleasure in being called a "bad contest surfer," thinking, "If a good surfer loses to a bad surfer in a contest, it's the fault of the contest, not the surfer." He smiled and walked away before the compliant and winning wanker held the trophy high.

Early Monday morning, he stacked all 11 of his free boards into his truck and delivered them to his sponsor's doorstep. From his savings he bought a used Thruster to complete a decent four-board quiver which included a broken and repaired Takayama noserider, a Fitzgerald Hot Buttered pin winger, and a more contemporary 8'10" Rawson gun. Surfing, which had become a boring job for the past three years, was fun again. Later that year, a photo appeared of him surfing without any stickers. His clothing sponsor fined him five hundred dollars. Free to think his own thoughts again, he realized that being a walking billboard was an insult to a human being. He emptied his closet and folded the pile of clothing neatly on the bed. Anything displaying the brand on the outside of the garment, he put to one side, those few items that were well made and had the label on the inside, he put on the other side. The ones with visible words or logos he took to Tijuana and distributed among the poor there. They knew how to look silly with dignity, maybe because they had not paid for the privilege.

His final act of defiance was to scrape all of the names off of his truck, even the one that had been riveted in steel by the automobile's manufacturer. For the first time in years, he felt that he really was free. He would surf where he wanted and when he wanted, and he would be owned by nobody. He rode some mushy beach breaks in front of his Mission Beach home, and something inside of him swelled with joy. He was riding for the feeling it gave him, not for the pleasure and profit of those watching him. Some of his friends wondered why he wasn't ripping as hard as he used to, but nobody said anything. Feeling hungry, he went to the local coffee shop, ordered a sandwich and a Coke, and sat at a booth, patiently waiting for his food to arrive. The land of the free had been purchased by big business, it seemed. A man with a head shaped like a jellybean ordered two burgers, jumbo fries and a large Coke. His T-shirt advocated action, but his body contradicted the slogan. A pasty wimp attempting a mustache wore a backward baseball cap that read "Navy Fighter Pilot." The name of a maker of dungarees was emblazoned on a kid's back in four-inch letters, as if the boy had been named for one of the twelve tribes of Israel. A woman walked in with twin white poodles named Nas and Dow, scrawny and dirty, it was a bad joke now. There were surfboard logos on many shirts, and hats proudly putting the name of one company or another on the forehead, like the mark of the Beast.

America, he thought, America is filled with very smart people and very silly ones. The smart people feed off of the silly ones like creatures in H.G. Wells, *The Time Machine*. The smart ones despise the silly ones, although they could not exist without them. The silly ones could exist without the smart ones, except for an artificial need to be associated with their products. The last time he had watched television he saw a show about American youth being in the throes of a heroin epidemic. Switching the channel, he saw a story about a scientist who made a monkey glow in the dark.

Having traveled extensively, Al knew that people were the same in Hawaii, Alaska, Australia and Omaha, Nebraska. He had recently decided not to be one of the silly ones any longer, and he knew that he was not shrewd enough to be one of the smart ones either. He wanted to surf, to work an honest job for an honest wage, and to live and die by his own ideas. He wanted to be himself. Why was that so difficult?

He gave the TV and the VCR to an appreciative neighbor. He threw the cell phone and the beeper into the trash. He played some CDs, but listened to no radio or TV, bought no newspapers, but purchased two boxes of books at garage sale for five dollars. *The Plague* by Camus, made a lot of sense to him. So did the words of Muhammad Ali, Ralph Nader, Ben Franklin, Steinbeck, CS Lewis and Jesus. He wrote his own thoughts on the kitchen wall:

Society is a drug addict; it's healthier without extra money.
A fat man in a Porsche is still just a fat man.
Hitler should have taken a closer look at Jessie Owens.

He grew as many vegetables as possible on the little space behind his house. At the grocery store, he avoided brand names and used beach sand and baking soda for his cat's box, rather than pay three dollars a pound for perfumed dirt. He took a job as a gardener, and fished or surfed in the mornings and the evenings. His parents, friends, girlfriends and sponsors all dropped him. He was weird, maybe crazy. But he didn't feel crazy. He felt like he was waking from a coma a little at a time. He lived alone and his house began to decay around him. His hair and beard were untrimmed, and his clothes became rags. Those who did not fear him, pitied him. Those who did not pity him, hated him. Everyone talked about how he had been a promising surfer, and could have grown into a good sales rep when he retired. What none of them could understand, however, was that he was completely happy for the first time in his life.

He paid his rent and left his little house on the 22nd of December. Then he took all of his savings, $1,292.47, from the coffee can in the back yard, and drove across the California border, into Mexico. The disease, he could see, had spread 100 miles into Baja, where everyone labored for things they did not need. The farmers and cattle ranchers of the old days had become the janitors and maids of the new days. He kept driving. One broken fan belt and three flat tires later, he came upon a cluster of wooden houses by the sea. The people there fished and grew corn. The children played on the dirt streets and everyone ignored the right point break and the thunderous beach break near the settlement. To them, the waves were merely obstacles to their livelihoods. To him, they were as honest and non-commercial as the people who watched them with fear and anguish, people who lived on the land and the sea, and who looked to the sky and the priests for signs of what was going to happen next. It offered him a good life, for about 20 years.

He should have warned them. The men that had been stuck on the dirt road in their European sedan wanted to buy just a little land for a road and a small hotel. Soon they needed more land, for a casino. Of course, there needed to be a shopping center and a discount clothing outlet. How else could they pay for the library, the school and the modern hospital that they were going to build for the people? It was all done on a handshake. The marina at the point was the start and finish of everything. When the reefs were dynamited, the shellfish all died. Next, the fishing dried up, and everyone worked for the hotel. The water was filthy, but tourists came down in droves to drink and play shuffleboard. Al had seen it all before, the disease that swept unsuspecting people into prosperity and misery and spiritual poverty. One day he drove up into the mountains, his worn out leather sandals stained with the blood of two decades of fishing and hard work, and his last remaining surfboard dinged and patched and broken and fixed twice, the foam rotten beyond repair. It had about one good swell left in it.

He moved into a small mountain village and took a Mexican wife. Most there consider him *loco*, because he speaks against progress. Some say that he is a communist. A few call him saint. He spends more time in the church than even the priest, praying for things that other people pray against. He was once overheard asking God to send a mighty hurricane, an earthquake, economic collapse, bugs to every computer around the world, confusion to all biotech engineers, and a flood to wipe out the new town that never did fulfill its promise of jobs, education and good health to the people. He prayed that nobody would be hurt by the natural disasters, but that the investors would leave the village alone, where time could heal it and bring it back to the way that it had been.

Al never goes to the movies. He refuses to even consider getting a computer. Once in a while, however, he finds an American newspaper, and he sees the advertisements for the clothing company that he abandoned decades earlier. From this angle, he can see people clearly. He feels sorry that they can't see what he sees—that they will be spending a lot of extra time at work in order to buy phones and games and clothing that will end up in a landfill in less than a year. Outside of his house, he hears children playing simple games in the dirt with a ball and a manzanita branch, faces caked with dirt, wounds open and dirty, returning to homes with dirt floors and stick roofs, waiting for the evacuation that the answered prayer of one big rain will bring. There must be a better life for them, he thinks. Perhaps I was wrong. His thoughts are disturbed by loud laughter, the type you don't hear in video arcades or daycare centers. The children laugh until someone is hit by a rock and then there is crying. A fight breaks out, and Al does nothing to stop it. He knows that there will soon be laughter again. The daylight fades into a long night filled with stars and silence. And what would they do with a better life? Al wonders as he drifts off to sleep, his youngest between him and his wife in a warm bed of straw laid on the floor. He touches the little boy's face with his hand, and curls up next to his wife, who moans seductively, and cuddles up closer to him, content with the food she has eaten that day, and the warmth of his body.

PAL AL, THE MAN AND THE LONE RANGER

In just over fifty years, Alan Nelson has lived everywhere from Mainland China to Costa Rica, mastered several languages, become a top-flight surfboard designer, an award-winning designer of small airplanes, a big-wave pioneer, an ace trial attorney and a hard-living partner of Bobby Patterson and Butch Van Artsdalen, who both died young. Now, he was taking it easy, running a job, building a home in Cardiff, California, getting fine work done ahead of schedule and riding waves whenever possible. Living next door to the building site were a 50 year-old man and his mother.

Al recognized him as an independent thinker, and often went to him for advice, although the rest of the world had branded the man, Mentally Retarded. Nobody but Mother had spoken to her boy for decades and the connections to his brain had grown so brittle that he rarely formed syllables any longer. That began to change when Al gave the man a hammer and a set of nail bags, which he wore to the job, and put away each night at the foot of his bed in a wooden toy box with The Lone Ranger, Trigger and Tonto, artfully painted on all four sides of it.

The man was up each morning before the construction crew arrived, watching the big trucks pull in with stacks of wood and bags of sand that were being magically transformed into a house. Every day at one o'clock, however, the man disappeared into his own house, to eat the deviled eggs and ham sandwiches that his mother had prepared and served on a cafeteria tray, leaving the boy alone to watch reruns of The Lone Ranger. He had seen every episode since his childhood, spending decades worth of allowance on comics of the Masked Man. He also had quite a collection of posters, black masks and toy white horses, which covered every corner of his bedroom.

While he had not been so much as a minute late in the three months of his employment, one morning the man didn't show up for work at all. Thinking that his friend might be ill, Al walked to the house at lunchtime, and peered through the dusty screen door, straining to see Donald Duck flash across the old, wooden TV set. "Come in boss," said the man.

Al walked into the dark room, letting his eyes adjust to see the man reclining on the sofa, still in his pajamas, with his lunch uneaten. He never turned to face Al, who took his place in a chair located in the corner of the room. "Are you sick?" asked Al.

"No," said the man, without diverting his attention from the TV set.

"Why weren't you at work today? We needed you."

Nothing was said, and Al and the man watched Donald Duck in an army uniform, making his usual mess of things, until one o'clock. "Time for The Lone Ranger," said Al. Without turning his eyes away from the TV, the man spoke. "There is no Lone Ranger. He's an actor that rides a white horse and then they put him on television. He isn't real, boss."

"Who told you that?"

"He did," said the man, motioning with his head, to a house four blocks down the street, where his only playmate, the young boy, lived. "There is no Lone Ranger, boss. Just an actor." There was no joy or sadness in the man's voice, and Al returned to work while the man sat on the couch drinking Pepsi by the quart and watching cartoons, talk shows and television evangelists. When Al returned that evening, the man was still seated alone, in front of the TV. This time, Al showed up with the man's favorite meal—cheeseburger and fries. The man picked at the fries, and Al noticed a stack of Lone Ranger posters that had been taken from the bedroom wall and were now piled up in front of the fireplace. The man looked into the TV set and repeated, "The Lone Ranger is not real, boss. He's not real. He's only an actor."

An entire week went by and the man never came to the job or even left the house. His mother made him food and then left for work, as her only son sat, watching Tom and Jerry, Lassie, M.A.S.H., My Three Sons, All in The Family, Gomer

Pyle USMC, Dragnet, Gilligan's Island, The Adventures of Scoobie Do, everything but The Lone Ranger. Each day, Al came by at lunchtime with food for himself and for the man, who continued to recline listlessly in his pajamas, on the couch. Al sat in his usual spot.

"I was over in the next valley," said Al. The man was unmoved, watching Green Acres, barely smiling at the appearance of Arnold the Pig, quickly returning to a blank expression after remembering what the boy had said, that it was a trick and that the pig could not really talk. "In the valley, I ran into a man on a white horse," continued Al. Now, for the first time in nearly a week, the man was curious. He sat up and looked at the boss. Was he kidding? No, Al was serious as he continued. "He said that the neighborhood is getting bad and that he needs your help to clean it up." The man sat up straighter, wanting to believe. But the proof given him by the boy had been strong, and was supported by the boy's mother and father who claimed to have seen the movie set where The Lone Ranger was filmed, in the hills behind Hollywood. Then again, Al had never lied to him. Confused by contradictory evidence, the man collapsed, hopelessly, back onto the couch.

The man returned to the TV screen and Al excused himself and made for the door. Suddenly, Al stopped in the doorway and turned back to the man. "I almost forgot; he told me to give you something." Now, the man sat bolt upright, watching as Al took a shiny object from his pocket. A silver bullet! The TV did not exist as the man concentrated on the bullet that Al turned over to him. Clutching the bullet in his hand, the man looked up, and said, "It's from him."

The man turned off the TV, changed clothes and returned to the job. That evening, The Lone Ranger was restored to his rightful place in his bedroom.

The next day, the man showed up for work early, but Al and the rest of the crew were late, out having breakfast. Then, the cement truck driver pulled up with a load.

The man, who could easily pass for a construction foreman in his new overalls, pressed denim shirt and sport's cap, glared at the driver. He had seen the boss do this a million times. "Bring 'er on back," he shouted, waving the truck in. Thinking that he was dealing with the foreman, the driver jerked it into reverse. The man never gave further instructions, and never even flinched until the truck disappeared in the ravine and the driver bailed out on the dirt, screaming at the man, but unharmed.

When Al and the crew finally showed up on the job, the big truck was in the big ditch, lying on its side. Then came another big truck to haul the cement truck back onto the street. A TV cameraman had questioned the excited driver about the incident. Next, they interviewed the man, who said only that the truck had gone over the cliff and that it wasn't his fault. When the man spotted Al, he left the camera crew who had been interviewing him and ran up to the boss, smiling, shouting, "Al, The Lone Ranger is real. He's real, Al."

Some time ago the man saved up his allowance and purchased a little glass case for the silver bullet. It remains on his nightstand to this day as a token, and all the proof he'll ever need that someone is watching out for him.

MEXICO ON FIFTY CENTS A DAY

On October 22, 1964, I became the first among my friends to achieve the status of legal California driver. That week my best friend Zero and I pooled our money and bought a 1954 Ford station wagon for one hundred dollars. For ten more dollars we bought a Pioneer eight-track stereo, complete with a James Brown tape. We spray painted yellow flames on the Ford's white fenders and were off, to Baja. Neither of us had ever crossed the border before, but we had heard about San Miguel, Three M's, Stacks and Hussong's Cantina. This was a distant land only a few hours from home. Four bald tires, no spare, no map, no insurance, ten or eleven wrinkled dollars between eight sandy pockets, plus an ashtray full of change. We had no idea of where we were going or how we'd get there.

We crossed the border, weaving through street vendors and crooked cops, and were soon driving the old mountain road that a rusty sign in Tijuana said led south, to Ensenada. After becoming increasingly loud in his suggestion that I was going the wrong way, Zero finally shouted that we were lost. "How do you know where we are? You've never been here before."

"There's no surf in the mountains, idiot!"

"If you don't like it, then you drive..." I said, half jokingly, letting go of the wheel and throwing my hands into the air.

The momentary distraction sent us off the road, and we flew into blackness, airborne for an eternal split-second. My short life flashed hard. I thought of my parents and my two little brothers, and of surfing, one wave in particular, a green, wind chiseled tube at Newport River Jetties that I had ridden, rather well I thought, a few weeks earlier. Everything told me that we were dead. Then, thud, we reconnected with the earth. In the time that it took to land, Zero had taken hold of my hair and was pulling it, yelling the word "idiot" over and over. He was still holding onto my hair, but it didn't hurt anymore. We were dead. I took a breath and my lungs filled with air. I was tingling and laughing and breathing in every ounce of life that I could taste.

We had only levitated a few feet, and landed hard against a huge bolder, one of few obstacles between us and the valley of the shadow of our death, one hundred feet below. Zero slowly let go of my hair, and started crying, laughing, hugging me, sorry that he had pulled my hair and called me an idiot. I was sorry that I had nearly killed us. We both laughed hard and got out of the car slowly, listening to the Ford creak as it sank deeper into the hillside. Zero hitchhiked back to Tijuana for help and I stood by the side of the road, keeping the car from dislodging through nothing but hope and prayer. Hours later, Zero returned with a man in a truck, a chain and two friends. Many hours later we were on the road again, no damage except a blown tire, that our new friends had replaced. They said that God had protected us, something I never doubted. Because we belonged to God, they would not accept the few dollars we offered for their help and the spare tire. They asked instead that we put money into the collection box at church and light a candle to the Virgin Mary for each member of their families, which were so big that the initial payment plan would have been less expensive.

The night ride was spooky now, clutching the wheel, seeing pretty homemade grave markers reflect our headlights, showing where others had been less fortunate than we had. It was late, and we were tired when we hit the coast that night, so we pulled over and slept in the back of the station wagon until dawn. Luck was strong again; we had blindly parked for the night directly in front of Three M's—nobody out, four to six foot, glassy walls.

We made camp on the dirt cliff above the break and then rode ourselves numb, wounded by rocks and urchins, sunburned and happy. Wanting for nothing but food, we drove to the nearest roadside taco stand and ordered a dozen carnitas. Two bucks filled us up. We surfed until our guts hollowed out again, then went back to the taco shop for another dirty dozen.

The assassin sharpened his knife and reached beneath the counter to bring up a hog's head—tongue swollen, ears hairy, flies eating the watery eyes. Hungry as we were, we bid him *no gracias* and headed for the town of Ensenada. After a few wrong turns we found a sacred shrine, a monument, a legend called Hussong's Cantina. Maybe they had food. They didn't. They had beer, and Zero had too many beers and began acting stupid like he always did when he was drunk, doing the Mexican hat dance on his new straw hat, crushing it with his foot at the conclusion of the dance. He was a stupid drunk, sometimes violent, once stripping down to his underpants at a party. I had to get him out of there before we were arrested. I drove him back to Three M's where I helped him into the tent. He pissed in his sleeping bag and snored like a pig.

Going through the wagon with my flashlight, looking for cans of food, I noticed that our duffel bags were missing. In them were all of our clothes, and the remaining cans of beans and soup and the loaves of bread that would keep us alive for the week. The theft cut our trip short. We drove carefully back home after riding the dropping swell the next morning in San Miguel, all the way home discussing our plans to return, better prepared, next week.

This time we had a spare tire, ten extra dollars and ate nothing from the roadside stands. We did, however, go back into Ensenada for hurachi sandals and a serape. Maybe a few skyrockets. We strolled through town, high on the feeling that only good waves can bring, and feeling secure because we had a little money in our pockets. We entered a shop, in search of cherry bombs. The shopkeeper asked us to follow him to his massive firecracker display, which stood proudly, adjacent to a wall of switchblades. As he walked ahead of us, I noticed something familiar about him. My corduroy dinner jacket! Of course it was his jacket now, just like it was his country, and there was nothing that I could do about it. I whispered the news to Zero. He laughed hard, until he noticed that the man's son was dressed in his pants and T-shirt, items liberated from us at the Hussong's parking lot on the previous weekend. Near the light and warmth of the campfire that night, filled with quarter tacos and dime Cokes, we realized that a few bags of clothing was a cheap price for all of this.

THE HEART OF A MAN

As I recall it was Tom who first met him on a diving trip to Pelelui where he had stayed with him and the entire Camacho family for three weeks. Tom decided to pay the family back for their generosity by bringing their oldest son, Robert Louis, to our home on the island of Guam. No Camacho had ever been off of their little island chain before. Now, a 17 year old boy named for the man who had written his father's favorite book, *Treasure Island*, had taken the big boat and the first step toward what we like to call civilization. Pelelui was half a century behind the industrially revolutionized hum of America in the 1970s, and the boy had grown up without things like Silly Putty, Hula Hoops or plastic handled six-shooters.

When we met him at the dock he was silent, looking beyond his coral-cut bare feet into the dirty water of the harbor. We realized later that he was afraid to speak or smile, embarrassed to reveal what a lifetime of chewing betel nut had done to his otherwise perfect Micronesian mouth. When Tom took him down the freight elevator, he clutched his arm like a child with a teddy bear, fearful because the floor below him was moving.

I got him a job as a gardener at the hotel where I worked as a waiter. Later, he was moved into a house that the hotel kept for their employees. During that first month, he was so quiet that we thought he knew no English. But soon he began speaking a quaint, easily understood form of pidgin English used throughout Micronesia. Before long he was talking about everything, mostly his island home, where he often speared sharks and other big fish. He talked about the way that he and the other boys in his village had their eardrums broken by the older divers when they were children, so that their ears would scar over and allow them to withstand the pressure of deep dives. Robert Louis could free dive to 70 feet, something that he was ashamed of, coming as he had from a place where all good divers could go down 90, or more.

Still, he was the best diver known to us, disappearing far beyond us, and the curtain of dark water, into the depths, once returning with an 85 pound tuna thrashing to free itself from the steel shaft of his homemade, wooden spear gun. After that I wanted no part of my store-bought metal gun, and asked that he make me one like his own. First, we had to find a tree with good hard wood. Then, he cut down the tree and began whittling the wood into the shape of a musket. Next, he forged a metal bottle opener into a trigger, and ingeniously completed the process, using various pieces of junk like an old bicycle inner tube. The thing looked like something out of the *Beverly Hillbillies*, but it shot straight, and I was able to land some big fish with it.

After a brief stint with homesickness, Camacho, as we called him, decided that he liked the conveniences of Guam and would stay there for at least one year. With the exception of the hotel elevator, he was not afraid of anything. Not fire coral, or sea snakes, or sea wasps or the hammerhead sharks that swarmed as thick as Micronesian roaches in the water on some days. He was a skilled spear fisherman, rarely missing the dime-sized kill spot of his prey, and always glad to share whatever he caught with the rest of us. He was a proud young man with only one black mark against him—no matter how he tried, he could never get deeper than 70 feet. He trained in the hotel pool where I timed him swimming underwater for well over two minutes. He sprinted on the beach, hyperventilated, and held his breath for four minutes at a time. He quit eating coconut crab, fruit bat and pork, and survived mainly on mangos and shark hearts, which he devoured, raw, before he took to cooking them whole on a stick over an open fire. He supplemented his diet with spoon meat coconuts, which he gathered daily by climbing the palms on the hotel grounds, shaking the trees back and forth, causing them to sway dramatically, before he jumped from one to the other. The Japanese tourists at the hotel loved the act, and he was soon hired by hotel management to perform near the pool, each evening in a grass skirt. After descending from 30 or 40 feet, he would open the coconuts with a machete, and bring them to the tourists who drank from them while Camacho danced to a conga drum and sang in his native tongue. With the extra money he made, he consulted a witchdoctor, and paid a vast sum to the woman, just before she was arrested for fraud. Nothing helped. He could swim down 70 feet and no further.

"I want you to take me to America, Crees. I have been watching television, and I have found out that there is a place in America called Medical Center. You will bring me there, and they will operate on me to give me a turtle heart," he said one morning.

"Camacho, Medical Center is only a television show," I said to him.

"No, I will go to America and find Medical Center and get the turtle heart, even if you do not help me to do it." ·

We argued about Medical Center and the turtle heart, and I soon realized that I was getting nowhere with him. I tried another approach. "Camacho, why do you want a turtle heart?"

"You think I am only a stupid island boy, but I have thought about this thing for a long time. Think about what I am saying, Crees. I cannot get an eel heart because it is too small. A tuna heart would cause me to be fast, but not so brave. I thought, maybe a shark heart. That would make me brave, but mean, like a shark, and then I would be in trouble from always biting people and maybe even biting Kojak when I am in America, and then Kojak would hunt me down to kill me. A turtle heart, you see. It would make me fast and brave and strong, and still nice, and I could dive more than one-hundred feet. Please, I never ask you for anything, Crees. Please, go with me to Medical Center for the turtle heart."

Nothing I said dissuaded him, and so I flatly stated that I would not accompany him to America. He flicked his knife and it stuck in the dirt between my feet, before he picked it up and walked away. After that he avoided talking to me for a while and he tried, without success, to get other Americans to take him to Medical Center for the new heart.

He came to me one day with a gift of betel nut and lime and a six pack of beer, and we were soon seated on the beach, talking and laughing. Slowly, he came to the point of his visit. He had seen surfing and he wanted to try it. The next day, I took him to the learner's spot, a mushy, rolling wave. He took one look at the Waikiki-type surf and shook his head. "No, Crees. This is not surfing. This is playing like children play in the hotel pool, with toys. I want to surf, to ride in the tube. Take me to a place where I can learn to ride in the tube." I told him that it was not safe to ride the tube on your first day, and that such waves were dangerous for inexperienced surfers. "Ah, Crees, you are disappointing to me once again," he said.

There are tubular places like the ones that Camacho wanted to ride on Guam, but they are crowded, with nasty bottoms, covered with sharp coral. Then again, Camacho was young, quick, brave and as coordinated as a spider monkey. Against my better judgement, I took him out to a mini Pipeline with a savage bottom. I decided to paddle him out, and put him well onto the shoulder, where I would push him into the smaller waves. Since most beginners think that they are in the tube most of the time anyway, my plan was to let him catch a few waves on the edge, and then tell him that he had been barreled.

Upon our arrival at the tube spot I noted a dozen others out, all decent surfers, good enough to get in the tube, something that Camacho was anxious to try. He was so excited that he had worn his trunks in the car. While I was changing in the public restroom, he took my board from the roof, and began paddling out. I called to him from shore. If he heard me he did not turn around.

Then I paddled out on the board that I had brought for him, and entered the lineup right as he was finding his way into the middle of the pack.

The sets were a solid six feet, top to bottom and spitting into the channel. Every longtime surfer on Guam had major coral cuts and even the most experienced among them dreaded going over the falls there. Someone caught a wave, got barreled and spat out, onto the shoulder where he fell, hit bottom and came up bleeding from the forehead. The surfer was shaken and paddled in. I figured that this would scare Camacho half to death, and put an end to it. I paddled into the pack to rescue him, but he avoided me, paddling to the inside. There, he paddled for a smaller wave and I watched helplessly as the strong-offshore wind pushed him over the top just as he was about to drop in. I caught the next wave, and rode it to the inside. I was paddling out in the channel when I saw him in position, stroking for the wave that he wanted. He missed that one too before it exploded on the inside reef.

I was seated next to him, yelling at him, dodging the sets and trying to get him to listen to me and paddle onto the shoulder. "No, Crees, that is not where the tube is. If you want to play like a child, riding baby waves you can go ahead, but I must have the tube!" He paddled back into the pack where there was respect from the others, mostly sons of soldiers, because Camacho was a native of Micronesia. Nobody said a word as he paddled for the next wave, his shiny brown skin tightening as he stroked into a beautiful, blue six-foot peak.

Camacho paddled as if he had the heart of a great white shark. He paddled like all great surfers paddle, with commitment and power, lacking only technical skill which caused him to move like a wounded fish, the type that are in danger of being eaten by predators. He continued paddling as the wave stood up behind him. I had never seen anyone catch such a wave on their first time out, but here was Camacho, coming together with the tube of his dreams.

Somehow he made the drop. He got to one knee,

got in the tube for a split second, got nailed and went over the falls. From behind I could see his body roll over a second time, and I prayed that he would not hit bottom. Long seconds passed and I paddled inside to find him. There were stories of surfers getting caught in underwater caves here, and the longer I paddled, the more worried I became, wondering if I was going to have to break his parent's hearts by telling them that their son had drowned while I was teaching him to surf. I heard him before I saw him, laughing and shouting, "I love the tube, Crees!" I love the tube."

I expected him to return to the lineup, but Camacho paddled into shore, satisfied. He never surfed or even spoke about surfing again, saying as he dried off that day, "Surfing is nice, but it is too easy. Already in one day I can ride the tube better than most, and it is enough for me. I don't want to keep riding the tube again and again, and maybe missing a lot of good days of fishing and working just so that I can go into the tube all of the time."

On our next day off, we drove to the far end of the island to a spot where we had been diving once before. While changing into our trunks, Camacho told me of a crazy man who lived in a cave nearby, and once took a shot at him. Months later, I read in the papers about Seargent Yokoi, the Japanese soldier who had been left on Guam like an unexploded land mine. Yokoi had heard that the war was over, but believed it to be Yankee propaganda. After his capture, he was taken home to Tokyo where he lived the life of a confused patriot, watching his people pledge their allegiance to tall, American-inspired buildings and new technology.

The diving was bad that day and for many more days in a row. Camacho was bored when he decided to visit his cousins in the Philippine Islands for a month. He was such a good and hard worker that the hotel gave him leave with half pay and the promise that he would get his job back when he returned. Upon his return he did not talk about diving or surfing or turtle hearts, but about the poor people in the Philippines and how many were finding poverty and drugs. "Even one time a man tried to get me to put a needle into my arm for drugs. When I said that I would never do that, he became angry with me, Crees. I hit him in the face, but he still tried to make me put the drugs into my arm. When he would not leave me alone, I told the police. Now this man is here, on Guam, with some of his family. I saw him today, Crees, and he said that he knows where I live and that he will come there at dark, only to kill me."

That night I took a baseball bat from the hotel, and followed Camacho to his home. He lived in a wooden shack with a Micronesian couple and their four children. We cooked the large fish that Camacho had speared, over a homemade rock fire ring. Micronesians are generally friendly, festive people, but on this night they only showed fear. The muddy road offered one way in and no way out. The shack was boarded up, and one at a time the residents kept watch from high atop a coconut tree. The children alone were without fear, making a game of standing watch. Unable to climb a coconut tree myself, I did my duty, sitting up in a wooden chair inside of the house, clutching the baseball bat, praying that I would not have to use it.

Morning was a gift to us all and joy returned to the shack as everyone ran out to pick wild fruits, wet from the night rain, from the jungle and Camacho and I drove off to work, laughing and talking. "You are my good friend, Crees. You have risked yourself for the life of me and of my friends. But if you have done such a thing for me, why then won't you come with me to America and to Medical Center for the turtle heart? You are not such a good diver and you should have a turtle heart for yourself. Since you have saved me, I will pay for your own heart, as a gift from me to you, Crees. Come, let us go to America. It is not so far away."

THE SEA HAGS

The Sea Hags are a part of an American tradition, direct descendants of Kerouac's On The Road, *prime candidates for Steinbeck's* Cannery Row. *Their hearts are as distant from the paid-to-look- pretty Surf Barbies of our time as their beloved Westport is from the air-conditioned luxury of a Waikiki surf vacation. They have lived simple, rewarding lives, and proven that adventure and individuality have not passed from our society, and are no respecters of gender. Self discovery has come with a price, but one that they would pay again and again, in order to live free and surf.*

It was raining, like it always did in Aberdeen, Washington. Hard, sloppy rain that turned sunny dreams into mud, when Cassie, Bobbie and Mishael, three 16-year old friends, crammed all of their belongings—clothing, sleeping bags and firewood, into the trunk of the 1975 Dodge Dart, and sat, car radio blasting, desperately wanting to go, but no idea to where. Since nobody had ever ventured far from town, and they didn't trust maps, they asked Todd, the 13 year-old boy next door that they sometimes babysat for, to drive them in the Dart to someplace nice. The boy, who could barely see over the dashboard, hit every bump in the road, but somehow safely deposited his friends onto the wet sands of Westport. Cassie took all of the change from the ashtray and pressed the two dollars and twenty-seven cents into the boy's hand. Then Todd drove his friendly captors to the bus stop where they waited until he found a ride home with a family friend. Not having to pay carfare, he returned half of the money in his pocket and was gone.

Big, stormy waves bounced off the jetty, forming ugly wedges as two surfers battled for position and a ride to shore. The girls had one surfboard and a wetsuit between them, and Bobbie was the first to suit up and paddle out, taking six feet of whitewater to shore, grinding to a halt when the fin hit the sand and her friends laughed and hooted. She stayed out for hours. Then it was Cassie's turn, then Mishael's. It was freezing and miserable, and scary being caught in the rips, but after those first waves, they knew that surfing would become their lives. They sat, wet, cold and happy in the Dart, watching the sky clear. That evening they made a fire, straightened coat hangers and cooked hotdogs. As they ate, Cassie and Mishael recounted their rides, and Bobbie paddled back out.

Bobbie was the talkative one, a natural born leader who had run for junior high school student body president with the charming slogan, "Vote for Bobbie, or die." It was at school that the budding junior politician met Mishael, a girl so shy that she kept her face hidden behind her coat, popping out with groundhog frequency to flick her dandruff, and watch it fall to the ground, like snow. While still in junior high, Bobbie met Cassie at a "Natural Helpers" retreat, where Cassie gave her new friend tips on dating 12th grade boys. Little by little the outcasts came together, bonded by their hatred of the dreary town whose main exports were lumber, desperation, *Suicidal Tendencies* and *Nirvana's*, Curt Cobain. There had to be something more than dripping fog and driving rain, or the ten days of sun shrouded in the haze of the pulp mills.

At first the girls survived on Cream O' Wheat, milk and fruit. When the money from their brief careers at Godfather's Pizza dried up, it went to Cream O' Wheat and water. Finally, it was water and the kindness of strangers, like big Al Pearly and his wife, Penny, the owners of The Surf Shop, who sometimes slipped a crisp hundred into a grateful hand. The night shift at Taco Bell delivered bags full of soggy burritos, after midnight.

Surfing was difficult under these conditions, but gradually each of the girls made their way to the outside break, where they rode set waves to the beach. While surfing and money don't often mix, Cassie launched an entrepreneurial plan. She would only drink the even number beers offered her, stashing the odd number beers behind the jetty, until she had accumulated an entire case of lukewarm Schmidt's, the brew that grew with the Pacific Northwest. The beers were sold from the Dart's trunk for a dollar each. With the money earned from this venture, the girls bought hotdogs, buns and a gallon-sized tin of chili beans. Condiments were lifted by the fistful from the Hungry Whale. The concoction was warmed on a borrowed hibachi, and sold for a buck-fifty. Just as business began to kick in, the cops threatened to shut them down, if they were caught.

Wooden crates discarded by the crab fishermen made huge bonfires, which attracted the attention of surfers and snowboarders from as far north as Seattle. Parties near the jetty raged until dawn. Each night the girls alternated between sleeping on the seats of the Dart and camping out on its roof. One morning, after a particularly hard night where they had tangled with a few of the local boys, the car was found covered with graffiti. The words, "Sea Hags," were the most prevalent. From then on they wore that title like a badge. They were the Sea Hags, a dedicated band of women surfer-skaters who didn't take crap from anybody.

The bonfires soon lured in Pete, Paul and Mike, three boarders from Seattle who became regulars on the weekends. They were janitors for Mervin Manufacturing, a thriving young corporation that produced some of the Northwest's best snowboards. The boys said that they could find jobs for the Hags, and that they could work along side them as janitors, at night. They would be free to surf and snowboard all day. Winter was coming, and the Dart wasn't getting any warmer. Nobody wanted to take the roof anymore, and there were skirmishes about who got to stretch out on the car seats. Illusionary photos from surf magazines soon entered the mix, and there was talk of going to Hawaii for the winter. Reality hit after counting the money from the "catering business," and coming up with a little over ten bucks between them. It seems that they had given away most of their food to hungry surfers and spent the profit on Schmidt's.

With no other options, they prepared for a job interview. Removing months of road dirt and saltwater, running a brush through dread locked hair, wearing their best jeans and newest T-shirts, three attractive young women emerged from the sand. That afternoon, there were numerous offers to move into houses owned by the local boys, who hardly recognized the upgraded Hags. Their last ten bucks went for gas.

Seattle was a world away, and they cruised the big city, Mishael nearly being abducted by gangsters, who tried to pull her into their lowrider before Cassie and Bobbie came to the rescue, Bobbie kicking a would-be assailant in the place that children come from. Now, where could this snowboard factory be? It occurred to them that the janitor gig might have been a line from some homeless skaters seeking a warm body for the night. They drove around until the car ran out of gas, and then pushed it onto a side street, jamming the parking meter with a Popsicle stick, in order to give themselves time to hunt down the work that they were now desperate for. Cassie eventually asked some street skaters for directions. Mervin was the big building that they had been circling for hours. The place covered half the block. This would be a good paying job. In the office the secretary rolled mascara-heavy eyes at the Hags when they asked for Pete, Paul and Mike. They were told to try again tomorrow.

Hope dimmed as the Hags curled up in the Dart for the night, parked on a busy street, and fought off starvation. They tried the factory again the next day. After a brief pause, the secretary did her duty by placing the call, then saying, "Mister Olson will see you now." Mister Olson, who turned out to be Mike from the bonfires, appeared from the double doors. What a great place, they even called the janitors, Mister. Cassie, Bobbie and Mishael followed Mike into an office where their old friends Pete and Paul were seated. The girls were offered pizza and coffee. Even as they ate, they were worried. The boys wouldn't have their jobs for long, all hanging around lazily, slurping coffee, choking down pizza, defiantly putting their feet on the big desk and generally trashing the place. It didn't register for some time—these were not janitors, but the owners of the hottest snowboard company in town. After stuffing themselves, the girls were directed to Mount Baker with new Lib Tech Snowboards, compliments of the boys at Mervin. Because of the pull of Pete, Paul and Mike they were given work as lift operators. Soon they had their own apartment, and enough money for regular meals. It snowed almost every day that winter, but it was the warmest they had been in years.

By winter's end, they had saved enough money to find their way to Hawaii. Surfing in the Islands, with warm water and no wetsuits was like a dream. Each day they improved, and rode bigger and bigger waves in places with pretty Polynesian names. With their enchanted surroundings came new challenges and adventures. The art of life was being perfected. And while they didn't realize it then, the Sea Hags were the latest to carry on a tradition started half a millennium ago by Kelea, the princess from Maui, who had sacrificed everything in order to surf.

Through it all the Sea Hags managed to finish high school and graduate with their class. Cassie and Mishael currently reside in Encinitas, California, where they share a home with their dogs, and surf nearly every day. Bobbie has moved back to Washington State.

TO ORDER SIGNED COPIES OF
JOYRIDES
GOOD THINGS LOVE WATER
KELEA'S GIFT
PLEASE SEND $14.95 PER BOOK
AND $3.95 S&H
CHECK OR MONEY ORDER TO:
CHUBASCO PUBLISHING
P.O. BOX 697
CARDIFF, CA 92007

INQUIRES:
CHUBASCO@COMPUSERVE.COM

TO ORDER MICHAEL CASSIDY'S ARTWORK
CONTACT:
WWW.SEVENTHHEAVEN.NET
760-806-7699

GUARANTEE

If you read this book and are unhappy, try reading it again, this time at the beach. If
you are still unhappy, pass the book on to a friend. If you have no friends, try to make
some. If you still have no friends, you have our personal lifetime Guarantee that you
will always be unhappy.